LOVE YOU TO DEATH, DARLING

BLAKE

Published by Blake Paperbacks Ltd
98–100 Great North Road, London N2 0NL, England

First published in Great Britain in 1992

ISBN 1 857820 12 6

British Library Cataloguing-in-Publication Data: A catalogue
record for this book is available from the British Library.

Typeset by BMD Graphics, Hemel Hempstead

Printed by Cox and Wyman, Reading, Berkshire

Cover painting by Christian Furr
Cover design by Graeme Andrew

1 3 5 7 9 10 8 6 4 2

To Rosie

...for just being herself

Acknowledgements

I have been given enormous help by a wide variety of people during the writing of this book.

In the UK I managed to speak to police officers, psychiatrists and other experts to try and get inside the minds of these killers. But, most significant of all, I talked at great length with Kathy Gaultney over two fascinating days in her cellblock at the Dwight Correctional Centre, in Illinois. It was thanks to her extraordinary insight into what it is really like to be convicted of murder, that I was able to grasp the full impact of why wives can sometimes be driven to wreak revenge.

Others whose assistance was invaluable include Suzy Davies, John Bell, Debbie Morse, Rosie Ries, Peter Wilson and, last but by no means least, Geoff Garvey.

In Los Angeles, Myra Kenley, Police Lt Fred Clapp and the staff of the UCLA research library were invaluable.

Finally, I particularly want to thank Mark Sandelson for his patience. Without access to his peaceful home in Beverly Hills, 90210, this book might never have been written.

WENSLEY CLARKSON 1992

WENSLEY CLARKSON

Wensley Clarkson, author of the UK national best-sellers *Hell Hath No Fury* and *Like A Woman Scorned*, is also a journalist, TV presenter and movie screen-writer. Since quitting full-time work on newspapers in 1987, he has produced television documentaries and is currently adapting one of his books, *Dog Eat Dog*, as well as another true crime project into film screen-plays for two major Hollywood studios. In 1991, he moved to Los Angeles with his wife Clare and their four children, Toby, Polly, Rosie and Fergus.

Foreword

In *Love You To Death, Darling,* I have tried to probe
the inner most feelings of the characters involved in
each of the awful crimes described here. My intention
is to give you a deep, unique insight into these killings
and perhaps some idea of why many marriages end in
bitterness.

Marriage is still supposed to be the most important
decision two people can ever make in their entire lives.
Divorce has been made more socially acceptable than
it once was. Yet the number of murders committed
by wives is definitely on the increase. So often, married
people trust each other without question and then
suddenly discover the sort of betrayal that can rip their
lives apart.

But what makes these crimes so terrifying is the cold
and calculating way they are committed. Wives are
frequently expected to be the stronger partners in any
marriage. But, is it possible that occasionally they
repress their feelings so much that their only means
of escape is to kill?

Perhaps some of the cases described here might hold
a few clues to this fascinating question.

I have interviewed countless people during the course
of my inquiries. But it was some of the defendants
themselves who really provided me with the ability to
delve inside these killers' minds and souls to explore
the motives behind each crime.

To present a series of crimes in such vivid detail might
upset those of a sensitive disposition. Be warned! I
have not held back in my quest to present every
possible detail — however disturbing. I have deliberately set out to inform and provoke in the hope that

next time such a crime occurs you will consider the motives behind it.

In trying to present the facts in this dramatic fashion, there is no doubt that some readers might discover discrepancies between my version of events and what has been reported elsewhere. I can assure you I have tried to use only information that I believe to be entirely accurate, but if I have erred in any way then it was entirely in good faith.

All these stories have been adapted to read as near to fiction as possible. That has meant I have had to make some informed deductions for dramatic purposes. But the actual facts of the cases are as they occurred.

Wensley Clarkson, 1992

*Previously published by
Wensley Clarkson*

Hell Hath No Fury
Like A Woman Scorned

Contents

1

In Cold Blood

St Jacob is the sort of place where nothing much happens. A sleepy little hamlet set in the middle of the Illinois flatlands, which many people describe as the heart of America. The population of this tiny community is just eight hundred and the locals have always said that they dread the day it tops the thousand mark.

As you drive into St Jacob you cannot help noticing the fertile fields that surround it on all four sides. Beautiful green pastures expertly farmed for maximum potential. They represent the real reason why the village even exists. The farming of land is the reason most of the population live and breed there — and that's the way they all want to keep it.

There are only half-a-dozen streets in St Jacob and they are never exactly bristling with traffic. There only ever seem to be a handful of pick-up trucks and the occasional car — and everyone knows the owner of each vehicle.

Perhaps not surprisingly, property prices in St Jacob have never been high. You could pick up a perfectly reasonable detached home on the edge of town for £30,000 — hardly a king's ransom by anyone's standards.

That was how Kathy Gaultney and her husband Keith came to settle in the town in the early 1980s. They had lived in larger communities nearby over the years, but both of them fell in love with the peace and quiet of St. Jacob — and houses went for a price even they could afford.

The problem was that neither Keith nor Kathy were working full time. He organised building site labour for construction sites all over the state of Illinois. But sometimes that could mean months of solid work followed by weeks of inactivity. Kathy — who had

9

just given birth to their son Walter — was not working at all. You could say the Gaultneys were struggling to survive. But at least they had their pretty little white wooden-slatted cottage in St Jacob — even though the modest mortgage repayments were proving very difficult to keep up.

It was fairly inevitable that Kathy had to get a job. She knew Keith was expecting it — and as their struggle to stay financially afloat continued, she came to the conclusion that any type of work would do. Within a few months of Walter's birth, Kathy Gaultney found herself working behind the bar at a rough and ready hostelry in nearby Collinsville. It wasn't exactly a well-paid position but it would keep the wolf from the door for the time being.

Back at home, Keith's work had completely dried up and he had taken to boozing excessively. There was a certain irony in the fact that Kathy's income came from serving alcohol and Keith was wasting all her hard-earned cash on the very same stuff. She was working all hours God could send while he knocked back countless bottles of rye at their pretty little home. Often she would arrive back late at night, completely shattered, only to find him slumped on their bed in a stupor.

At first, Kathy decided to bite her lip and say nothing to her husband. After all, he had been the breadwinner for many years before it had all turned sour. Things would pick up and he would sort himself out, she kept telling herself. The truth was that Keith Gaultney had long since given up the fight. His pride had taken a huge knock and now he was sinking rapidly into alcoholic oblivion. He did not really care any more. Just so long as Kathy kept working they could just about survive — and that would do him just fine.

When Kathy Gaultney met Mary O'Guinn one night

as she was serving beers behind the bar of the hostelry, she was at an all-time low. The mortgage had not been paid for three months. She could barely afford to clothe their baby son and 11-year-old daughter Rachel from an earlier marriage. Times were pretty desperate and she was not bashful about admitting it to anyone who would listen. It was a plea for help. Kathy knew full well that time was running out unless she could find some other, more profitable way of earning a living.

And Mary O'Guinn appeared like some angel of mercy — the answer to those desperate dreams. The attractive redheaded housewife was fully aware of how vulnerable Kathy was and she made her an offer she could not really refuse. On the surface it sounded like the opportunity of a lifetime.

Within a few weeks of that first meeting, Kathy and her equally stretched pal Martha Young were the proud owners of the New Way Toning Salon for housewives, in Collinsville. No-one questioned the women's sudden ability to pay tens of thousands of dollars in cash for the premises needed to house the club. But then only Kathy, Martha and their new best friend Mary O'Guinn were aware of the secret office hidden behind the gym.

In it was an assortment of weighing machines — but these had nothing whatsoever to do with keeping people fit. They were small scales which were perfect for weighing drugs before distributing them to a network of suppliers throughout the American mid-West. Kathy Gaultney had just become a full-time employee of one of the country's biggest drug cartels.

For the first few months, life at the New Way Toning Salon was very very good for Kathy and her pal Martha Young. The two women really looked and acted the part of bosses of a health club. Both of them looked like ordinary suburban housewives. Kathy, with her glasses and neat, short hairstyle always dressed

11

in a tracksuit and sneakers. She could have been any one of a million hardworking women in a middle-class enclave anywhere in the Western World.

And, perhaps surprisingly, the legitimate business was actually doing quite well. They had worked very hard to build it up. They had something to prove to Mary O'Guinn. For both Kathy and Martha rather looked down on the drug dealing that was going on in their backroom. But they also knew that without the narcotics gang behind their little venture it would have been nothing more than a fantasy for the rest of their lives.

Kathy tried hard not to consider the consequences of all those millions of dollars' worth of cannabis that were weighed, re-weighed and then packaged up for distribution among the street dealers of Illinois. She turned a blind eye when heavy-set characters used to turn up with vans for delivery and collection at all times of the day and night. Kathy was just delighted that for the first time in her adult life she had enough money to pay the mortgage, feed and clothe her children and enjoy some of the better things in life.

When Mary O'Guinn and her brother Roy Vernon Dean asked her if she would begin delivering some of the cannabis herself, she agreed because they were offering her more money to do it. And, with the drunken Keith now hitting rock bottom back at home in nearby St Jacob, it seemed to make a lot of sense. Kathy was actually starting to enjoy life again. There was something quite exciting about taking risks. There was also something very fulfilling about being able to spend all the money you wanted. Becoming a drug courier wasn't so bad after all.

Even when Kathy Gaultney found herself driving hundreds of thousands of dollars' worth of cannabis plus $45,000 in cash in the boot of her car, it did not worry her. Who would bother stopping and searching a housewife from St Jacob? She hardly looked the part of a hardened drug smuggler involved in one of the biggest cannabis supply networks in American criminal history.

As she parked her car outside her cosy little cottage in that tiny rural community, she did not even bother to take her valuable booty inside the house. It was better if she kept it out of the way of her kids and husband Keith. He was always ranting in redneck fashion about how awful drugs were. He even warned her daughter to be careful.

"There's a lot of evil people out there who'll try and force you to take drugs. Just tell 'em no way."

Keith Gaultney could hardly talk. He could not even come to terms with his own addiction — to alcohol. Yet somehow — in his mind at least — the damage he was inflicting on his own liver was not as morally wrong as smoking pot. Sometimes Kathy Gaultney felt like telling him that pot was probably less harmful that booze, but she never bothered. He would not have appreciated her opinions. As far as Keith Gaultney was concerned, women were to be seen and not heard.

"Kathy. What the hell have you got in the trunk, woman?"

Keith Gaultney was sober for once. But then it was seven in the morning when he went outside to get a jack from his wife's car and discovered a small fortune in drugs stashed in the boot.

Kathy Gaultney did not reply at first. She needed a moment to think about this. She was in a classic dilemma — did she admit to Keith that they were drugs, or should she try and deny they even belonged to her?

But it did not take her long to realise there was no point in hiding the obvious. Kathy pulled her husband down on the bed beside her and started to tell him the truth. But being honest is not always the best answer when it comes to marriage. Keith Gaultney was spitting mad. In any case, for once in his life, he had something on her. All his years of heavy drinking had put him in a vulnerable position as far as their relationship was concerned. Now, for the first time, he had the upper hand and he was determined to milk it for all it was worth.

"Drugs? What the hell are you doin' selling drugs?"

But then Kathy had the perfect excuse.

"How else were we goin' to pay the mortgage, the bills, the kids' clothes?"

Keith Gaultney did not like facing the realities of the situation. He hated the fact that he had not been the main breadwinner in the family for a long, long time. Kathy was making him face facts — and it hurt.

"But we could have survived some other way."

Kathy Gaultney did not agree. It was time for some plain speaking in that household. Maybe the discovery of the drugs was a blessing in disguise. Perhaps now she could come out in the open and say what she had been thinking for years.

"There was no other way. You've lived off my money for months. I haven't noticed you complaining."

Keith Gaultney did not reply. He understood her point but he would never accept that selling drugs was the answer. He'd never felt the urge to even try pot as a kid. Now his wife, the mother of his only son, was admitting that she was heavily involved in a vast drug ring. Keith Gaultney retreated into his own shell-like existence from that day onwards.

For months he hardly spoke to his wife and sank deeper and deeper into an alcoholic abyss. The only times he could bring himself to talk to her were when he could not stand the thought of what she was involved in. Then he would let fly with a tirade of abuse centred around the inevitable subject of drugs.

"How can you sit there and tell me that drugs don't harm people? How can you?"

Keith Gaultney was off again on one of his regular ranting matches with Kathy. But this time she decided to respond. She was fed up with him going on and on about drugs. It was time for some home truths.

14

"Well, pot is hardly any more harmful than all that booze you drink."

Kathy was hitting back. Okay, she could not defend the use of heavier drugs, but as far as she was concerned her narcotics overlords were only dealing in cannabis. Where was the harm in that?

But her husband did not quite see it that way.

"Drugs are drugs. One type leads to another. It's as simple as that."

Kathy was concerned about her husband's attitude because he was unshakable. Nothing would convince him that pot might not be so bad. She feared that he might one day do something about her involvement with the notorious Dean family.

But it wasn't just drugs that were tearing the Gaultney family apart. Keith's drinking had become a morning, noon and night-time obsession. The only work left to him was the opening of bottles. His reward — consuming the contents.

By the time Kathy got home after a hard day running the beauty salon followed by hours of weighing a fortune's worth of cannabis, she was exhausted. Yet, she would be expected to make them all dinner. Bath her son. Get both kids to bed and attend to her husband's every whim and command. It was simply proving too much for her to handle.

Some nights she would stay on at the shop in Collinsville and have a drink with her great friend and partner Martha, because it was infinitely preferable to going home to face Keith and the kids.

But Kathy knew things could not just go on like that for ever. When she got home late yet again one night in February, 1988, Keith rounded on her and started threatening her. She decided she'd had enough.

As Keith ranted and raved about "those damn drug peddlers", she packed a suitcase, grabbed both the kids and headed out the front door. A few days later, she filed for divorce. But what disturbed her the most was that each time she tried to have a sensible conversation with Keith on the phone, he would start up again about those drugs. But this time he was more adamant.

"I reckon the authorities would like to hear all about those scumbags you work for."

Kathy did not like the sound of what she was hearing. The ramblings of a drunken, vindictive husband were one thing. But a threat to destroy everything she had built up so carefully was another matter altogether.

She could sense from the tone of his voice that he was contemplating taking this whole business a much more dangerous stage further.

"It's the perfect weapon for a single lady."

The assistant in the gun shop in Collinsville might as well have been trying to sell Kathy Gaultney a piece of jewellery. But then that's America for you. A reasonable gun costs about the same as a nice ring. And it's just as easy to buy!

By then Kathy was looking at purchasing a .22 "Saturday Night Special". In a country where some states have more deaths from gunshot wounds than car crashes, it's no great surprise when a woman walks into a shop wanting to buy a gun.

As she handled the snub-nosed pistol over the counter of the shop, she knew she had to buy it. The stress and strain of running a legit beauty salon and an illicit drugs factory, and contemplating a divorce from her alcoholic husband was driving her to consider desperate measures in order to maintain the happiness she so needed.

"Do ya think it'll make my husband stop abusing me?"

It seemed a strange question to ask a guy who was trying to sell you a gun. But Kathy wanted some reassurance.

"I can assure you ma'am that no husband in his

right mind will mess with one a those things."

By the time Kathy Gaultney enrolled at a nearby shooting range for expert training on how to handle that gun, her husband's threat to blow the whistle on her illegal activities was constantly ringing in her ears. She did not know if he would carry it through or not, but she wanted to be prepared just in case he really did. No-one was going to destroy her life. She would see him go to hell rather than allow him to get away with ruining everything for her and the kids.

Back at their little house in St Jacob, Keith Gaultney was becoming a very lonely, isolated character. Kathy and the kids had moved out to live in Collinsville. He had no company. His only conversation was with a near-empty bottle. Perhaps it was not really that surprising when his addled, paranoid mind convinced him that the way to get Kathy back was to blow the whistle on those evil drug barons who had destroyed their life together.

Keith Gaultney picked up the phone and dialled the directory inquiry service.

"Internal Revenue Service, please."

He only meant to scare Kathy into seeing sense and coming back with the kids. The IRS would rap her on the knuckles and then go after the really big boys. Keith Gaultney did not even consider the fact that the US Drug Enforcement Agency would automatically get involved.

March 18, 1988, seemed like a pretty ordinary day at the New Way Toning Salon in Collinsville. There was a handful of women customers going through their $20-a-head skin-toning session, and no sign of the illegal activities that were a daily routine in the backroom of the premises.

Neither of the women even noticed the black van parked up across the street from the beauty salon. But they certainly realised something was wrong when

17

six Drug Enforcement Agents rushed through the front and back exits. Kathy's first reaction was to deny any knowledge of the drug den hidden behind the main store. Under her breath she muttered: "You bastard, Keith. You bastard."

As the well-dressed officers made a clean sweep of the premises, Kathy and Martha looked on with blank expressions. But beneath their surprised faces lay a fury that was virtually uncontrollable. Kathy looked over at her friend and said:

"That shit. I could kill him."

By the time the agents had taken away various bits and pieces of evidence of the drug packaging that was taking place behind the salon, Kathy was steaming mad. She had to get even — somehow.

"I know you did it, Keith. I just know."

Keith Gaultney hardly even bothered to deny it either.

As his wife tried to extract a confession from him that he had sparked the DEA raid that morning, he just let it all hang in the air. But his refusal to admit it just helped convince Kathy that there had to be a way to stop him before he destroyed everything she had built up so carefully.

Her drug bosses were not that worried by the raid because the agents could not find any actual narcotics. They decided that Kathy and Martha would have to continue dealing from their cars or homes rather than using the backroom of the salon. The two women really had little choice in the matter as they both desperately needed the money to survive. There was no turning back.

But there was a very real danger that Keith Gaultney would stir up even more trouble for his wife, especially since the whole of St Jacob now knew from local newspaper reports of the raid that his wife was a suspected drug peddler.

All it needed was another call from him to the

IRS and then Kathy's world would well and truly come tumbling down like a pack of cards. But Keith Gaultney was satisfied for the moment. He genuinely hoped that his wife would stop her involvement in drugs after the raid on the salon. But Kathy was in way too deep.

And she had already devised a plan to keep a much closer eye on her informant husband.

Keith Gaultney was delighted when Kathy announced she was moving back in and putting the divorce plans on ice. He actually believed that her decision was evidence in itself that he had done the right thing by informing on her to the authorities.

For the first few months after she reappeared, he even tried to slow down his drinking so they could resume a normal family life together with the kids. They actually seemed to start enjoying each other's company again.

Kathy wondered whether she had been wrong to condemn Keith in the first place. Maybe he wasn't so bad after all.

But soon his own self-doubt began to return and the booze battled its way back into a dominant position in his life once more. Many believe it was brought on by the reality of the situation that Keith found himself facing — his wife was even more heavily involved with the Roy Vernon Dean drug cartel than before. Now she was delivering vast quantities of cannabis around the county. If anything, she was in much more deeply than before.

"I told you to stop dealing drugs, Kathy. I won't have it."

Kathy Gaultney tried to humour her husband by promising that she was not involved any more. But he knew she was. Mind you, it was the only way they could scrape together enough money to survive.

"Drugs are going to be the death of us, Kathy. You mark my words."

Keith Gaultney had a habit of putting his foot in his mouth. But this time he was putting ideas into his wife's head. She looked over at him, droning on and on through the alcohol, and thought about that Saturday Night Special she purchased even before the DEA raid on the salon.

She knew she could not bear the thought of listening to his drunken accusations for much longer. Something had to be done to silence him for ever. But it wasn't until almost a year later that Kathy Gaultney actually built up the courage to shut him up for good. They had many "near misses" — with Keith threatening to go to the authorities virtually each time she came home late. But somehow he kept quiet, although the ranting was becoming less and less coded. Now he was getting pretty blunt.

"One day, I'll go to them and then that'll stop that bastard Dean."

Kathy knew all the danger signs were there. She had to do something before it was too late.

Rachel was delighted when her mom told her and a friend to "get lost" for a few hours on the evening of September 22, 1989. St Jacob was the sort of place where kids could safely play on the streets until all hours.

But there was one small problem. Neither Rachel nor her pal had any money and they wanted to go down to the late-night store and buy themselves some sodas and a packet of potato crisps.

So the two girls sat down in the empty breaker's yard opposite their house in Second Street and waited for Kathy Gaultney and Rachel's half-brother Walter to leave on a shopping expedition. The plan was to then slip in and steal a few dollars from Keith Gaultney's wallet. He was always so far gone on booze by about seven that he'd have long since collapsed in bed, out to the world.

But as the two girls waited patiently for Kathy to

leave the house, they could not possibly have had any idea what was happening inside.

Kathy Gaultney looked down at the snoring man who called himself her husband and sneered. As he lay there in his drunken state, she felt no qualms for what she was about to do. She had locked her son out of the bedroom and told him to wait in the hall before they went shopping. Now she had some unfinished business to attend to.

The .22 Saturday Night Special was rock steady in her hand. Just seeing him there in that comatose state convinced her that what she was about to do had to be right.

She cocked the gun, leant down silently and pressed the barrel right into the fatty folds of skin on his forehead. Still he did not stir. Even with the ultimate killing machine pointed right into his head, he could feel nothing because of all the booze he had consumed.

She prodded the barrel one last time just to see if he would notice. But there was nothing there. Perhaps if he had stirred then Kathy Gaultney might not have seen it through. But somehow she imagined he would hardly feel a thing because he was already out cold anyway.

As her finger tightened its grip on the trigger, she placed her left hand over the gun to help steady it. She did not want it rebounding back on her. All those lessons at the gun club had given her a good basic knowledge of the mechanics of guns.

Now it was time. She pressed hard and felt the gun tremble as it fired. The bullet went through his head in a split second. But he was no longer asleep. The full force of that bullet had somehow awoken him from his drunken stupor.

For a moment, Kathy was taken aback. She had not expected this by any means. With the gun still firmly in her hands she pulled back a few inches and aimed again at his head. This time it would have to work.

In those few moments between shots, her eyes explored every inch of his body, trying to establish whether his apparent consciousness was just a passing phase. But she could not take any chances. She fired again from close range. This time the bullet tore a gaping hole in the side of his head and took off on a helter skelter of a ride around the inside of his brain.

Without even a flicker of emotion, Kathy Gaultney pulled out a drawer from the chest next to the bed and dropped it onto her husband's corpse. It seemed the perfect way to make sure it all looked like a robbery that had gone tragically wrong.

Ten minutes later she was leaving the house with her young son, completely unaware that her daughter Rachel was lying in wait across the street.

Rachel and her pal crept in the back door of the house in silence just in case they awoke Keith Gaultney. The youngsters opened the door to the bedroom like two cat burglars on the prowl.

When she looked inside that bedroom where her step-father lay dead, she had no idea of the brutal killing that had just taken place. No-one knows if there was even a flicker of life left in his body when she snooped around the room looking for his wallet. But one thing is sure — she took no notice of the drawer emptied over his body. It was all pretty much par for the course for the ever-drunken Keith Gaultney.

Once she found what she was looking for, Rachel left the room, completely unaware that she had been just a few feet from the body of her dead step-father.

But the timing of her secret snoop around that room was to be the crucial evidence in convicting her own mother of first-degree murder.

"Is that the police? My husband's been shot. You better come quickly."

Kathy Gaultney sounded distraught to the telephone

operator who took her emergency call later that evening. She told officers she had returned home from late-night shopping at a number of local supermarkets to find her husband shot dead in their bed. It seemed like a robbery that had gone terribly wrong.

As the paramedics, medical examiners and assorted police milled around the Gaultney house, one figure stepped back into the shadows and found herself examining her own conscience — Kathy's 13-year-old daughter Rachel.

For she had witnessed her mother leave that house with her half-brother and she had seen what later transpired to be the body of her step-father. Basically, this scared young girl was withholding the key to his murder and she just did not know what to do.

While the flashing lights of the police cars disappeared into the distance some hours later, she retired in silence to her little bedroom, haunted by the role she had played in the whole tragic scenario.

It was only a few weeks later that Rachel decided to call the police and tell them what had happened that fateful night. Detectives later admitted that without her testimony it is entirely possible that Kathy Gaultney might never have been arrested.

For those first few weeks after the murder of her husband, Kathy Gaultney cut a pretty confident figure in St Jacob — still reeling from the first deliberate killing in its hundred-year history.

People may have been whispering behind her back, but Kathy did not care. She had got rid of her drunken, nagging husband and that was all that mattered in her mind.

Even when a friend advised her to contact a lawyer just in case police tried to haul her in for questioning, she was super cool about the whole business.

In fact, when she motored into nearby Edwardsville with a friend one morning, she did not feel in the least bit threatened by the vicious gossip that was sweeping the area about her involvement in Keith's death.

As she slowed down at a crossing, she even smiled when she spotted two state police detectives and an attorney leading the investigation into her husband's murder.

"Aren't you guys having a busy day?"

Kathy Gaultney really was pushing her luck. Here were the top law enforcement officers involved in her husband's case and she was ribbing them mercilessly.

Unfortunately, what Kathy Gaultney did not realise was that the case against her was now sufficient to warrant her arrest. A few minutes later, police pulled up the van she was travelling in and arrested her for the murder of her husband.

In April, 1990, Kathy Gaultney, aged 34, was sentenced to life imprisonment after being found guilty of the first-degree murder of her 35-year-old husband.

Prosecuting attorney Don Weber told the court: "This crime was planned, but it wasn't planned well."

And, describing Kathy Gaultney's own daughter's role in her mother's conviction, he added: "In any crime, the inadvertent witness is the one thing you can't plan for."

Some months after her trial, Kathy Gaultney contacted authorities and agreed to provide inside information on the drug cartel she worked for with Martha Young.

Twelve people, including Mary O'Guinn and her notorious one-legged drug baron brother Roy Vernon Dean, were arrested and eventually given very lengthy sentences for their involvement in one of the biggest narcotics rings in US history.

Martha Young was also imprisoned as a result of testimony from her best friend Kathy. But, amazingly, the two women still write to each other from their respective prisons in Illinois and Gaultney says that they have remained friends despite everything.

24

Meanwhile Gaultney herself insists that she did not carry out the murder of her drug informant husband. She maintains that he was killed by other members of the Roy Vernon Dean gang who wanted to silence Keith Gaultney before he helped authorities close down their drug cartel.

When I interviewed her in the notorious so-called "women killers' cottage" in the grounds of the Dwight Correctional Centre in January, 1992, she was still protesting her innocence and insisting that she would eventually succeed in overturning the jury's verdict.

In a hushed voice, as various other inmates walked freely around the inside of the stone-built building, she told me: "I put up with a lot of shit from Keith but there's no way that I killed him."

As one woman inmate — imprisoned for life for murdering her parents — poured us each a cup of tea, Kathy went on: "I've done a lot of bad things in my life, but I ended up paying the price for working for an evil ring of drug smugglers. They killed Keith and then managed to get the police to arrest me. One day I'll prise out the truth."

Meanwhile, Kathy continues passing her days reading and cooking inside one of the strangest cottages that I have ever visited. It remains to be seen if her desperate attempts to appeal against her sentence will ever actually be heard.

Having spent two fascinating days inside one of the world's most daunting prisons, I have to admit that Kathy Gaultney has a great deal of charm and intelligence. When she is eventually released, I have no doubt that she will successfully reinstate herself into society.

2
Poetic Justice

Paul Birch loved his job. Each morning he would walk briskly across the road from his neat suburban home in Kingston, Surrey, to his office just a few hundred yards away. It was so much more pleasant than facing one of those long traffic-congested journey or sardine-packed train rides into London.

The work itself was an art form, according to Paul. A carefully nurtured skill that took years and years of training. Now, at 33 years of age, he was at the peak of his profession. Each of his customers was a fresh challenge that had to be faced with equal enthusiasm.

Paul was also very proud of his job. He saw it as a vital service to the community and, in many ways, it was hard to disagree with him. But then embalming is one of those professions that many people would rather not hear about or see too much of. Even in these modern times, attitudes towards death are still tinged with fear despite the fact that it happens to us all in the end.

As one prominent member of the undertaking trade once said: "This is the only business in the world where everyone is a potential customer."

Paul himself had a definite way with people — both dead and alive. An unassuming, prematurely balding man with soft brown eyes and a very gentle manner, he had a reputation amongst local funeral parlours as being one hell of a good professional. He really did seem concerned that those grieving loved ones were treated with warmth rather than distance by their undertakers.

A lot of his colleagues put all this down to the fact that he had not taken the traditional route to the funeral business, which is filled with families that go back three, four, even five generations. No, Paul

26

Birch had even enjoyed a spell in the army before buying himself out in 1979. He had, as they say, lived a full life, and many believed that made him all the more sensitive towards his clients.

Paul explained his unusual choice of a second career by saying he had always been fascinated by the "business" and he saw it as a genuine service to the community. He was delighted when he qualified as an embalmer and joined the prestigious British Institute of Embalmers at the tender age of 26. It had taken him just a year of careful training to reach that first step in his ambitious career in the world of death.

Throughout all this there was his gregarious, bubbly hairdresser wife Julie. They had first met when he was stationed in West Germany in the forces. Paul was just 24 years old and she was twelve years his senior. But none of that mattered. They had been instantly attracted. Julie's stunning West Indian looks were quite an eye-opener in the grim Bavarian countryside where Paul was based at the time. Soon she was teaching Paul things about lovemaking that he never knew existed.

Julie — or "Beulah" as her family had christened her — was a very experienced woman in every sense. She had been married before and was the mother of three children, but she still retained a sense of fun that Paul had never come across before. She had a live-for-today attitude that he found truly magnetic. Happiness was her main priority. She desperately wanted to make Paul equally content.

When Paul quit the services, they soon settled in a modest, but very comfortable flat in Horace Road, Kingston. He pursued his career in the funeral business and Julie made great inroads into the hairdressing profession and was soon managing the B. Casual salon on the nearby Cambridge Housing Estate.

Horace Road was a pretty stodgy street when it wanted to be. Your run-of-the-mill lower-middle-class assortment of houses and flats built mainly between the wars. A breeding ground for die-hard bigots.

The sight of the handsome young man and his much older, West Indian wife was hardly greeted with enthusiasm by the locals. Many neighbours fully expected calypso parties and cannabis plants in the garden. The truth was that Julie and Paul were a rather charming couple who got on with their lives in a very hardworking, studious sort of way. Both of them were up early every day, worked long hours and came back to the flat to enjoy romantic candle-lit dinners before retiring to bed for an early night.

To start with, hardly any of the neighbours even said good morning as Paul and Julie ventured out on their way to work. But gradually they became accepted by the other residents, much to their surprise.

But being involved in a mixed-race marriage taught Paul a lot more about life. It opened his eyes to the short-sighted prejudices that exist and it sparked his interest in local politics. You see, Paul Birch wanted to do his bit to change the world. He began to nurture great political aspirations, and they soon manifested themselves in his application to join the local Labour Party.

But he did not stop there. Next he put himself up for election to the local council and, in an area that included a couple of vast council housing estates with high rises, he easily got in. Within a few years of arriving in Kingston the Birches had become a very well known local couple. Soon their black and white "coalition" seemed irrelevant. By 1986, they were seen as a very glamorous pair. Now it was more than just their neighbours who were greeting them in the street.

Throughout all this, Paul also managed to build his reputation as one of the finest embalmers in Surrey. His job at the Lear of London firm was pretty unique because he was given the official title of "mobile embalmer." In short, wherever there was a corpse that needed attending to, Paul Birch, complete with radio pager, would be sent.

He prided himself on his ability to "rebuild" the most horrifically injured bodies to their former glory, so that loved ones could take one last look at their deceased relatives and know they were going to a better world looking fit and healthy enough to be accepted.

Paul appreciated just how important it was to make those corpses look almost as good as new — even though they were more often than not only laid out for a few hours before being lowered to the ground or turned to ashes for eternity.

His bosses at Lear were delighted that Paul's political career was going so well. They saw his success as a great way to spread the word about the funeral business. Bring it more out in the open for everyone to see and hear about.

And when Paul announced he was standing as the Labour Party candidate for Kingston in 1986, they were over the moon. The undertaking business had always been hidden behind blacked-out shop windows and talked about in hushed whispers. Now here was a man standing on a platform telling the world that he was an embalmer — and proud of it!

Sadly, Paul Birch's bid for real political power failed when he lost out to the Tory opposition. But at least he had made his mark on local party politics. He had become a real force to be reckoned with.

Meanwhile, attractive Julie was busy behind the scenes working at her hairdressing salon and returning home each night to make her man feel happy in every way possible. And Julie knew that the best way to a man's heart was through his stomach. She loved cooking huge stews and rice dishes that he had grown to really enjoy.

But over the road from their neat little flat, Paul Birch was juggling more than just his career as an embalmer with those deep-set political aspirations.

29

His recently discovered local fame had put him on a pedestal at Lear's of London — and for the first time in his life he was attracting the sort of attention only unmarried men are supposed to revel in.

Their rubber-gloved hands just brushed each other ever so slightly. Through that white see-through material it might have meant nothing. After all, they were just about to carry out a full embalmment on a body that lay on a slab in front of them. Then he caught her glance and realised exactly what was going through her mind.

But still he said nothing and — like the true professional he was — he started the gruesome task that lay before them. As they moved the corpse over on its stomach her eyes caught him head on again. Paul Birch coughed. It was a sign of embarrassment really. He wanted to somehow let her know that he knew. But he did not really know how to handle the situation. However, he was fully aware of one thing — if Julie ever found out, she would become insanely jealous. He had never forgotten how she warned him once that if he was ever unfaithful she would "shoot your balls to bits."

Most women might not have meant it. But Julie was not like any other female he had ever met. Somehow, he suspected that she meant every word.

Despite his wife's warning ringing in his ears, Paul Birch was finding it very difficult to resist his colleague. It is probably hard to imagine how anyone could find such grisly surroundings in the least bit romantic, but when you've worked under such circumstances for many years you become immune to the smell and feel of a corpse.

As Paul Birch started blocking up the orifices that lay before him, he could not get his mind off that work colleague. He knew it would only be a matter of time before something happened between them. He could not help himself. He had to have her.

* * * *

"Who is she?"

Julie Birch did not beat about the bush. She was sitting opposite her day-dreaming husband at home a few weeks later when she confronted him head on. Julie was a woman led by her instincts and she knew her husband was falling for someone else. She had seen it happen before in her previous marriage. She was only too well aware of the signs: the distant responses, the late nights at work, the strange phone callers that hung up whenever she answered.

But Paul Birch was not ready to confess. He had only just met this other woman and he was not about to sacrifice eight years of happy marriage for the sake of some passing love interest.

"You bastard. I know there's another woman."

Julie Birch could not have been more blunt. She was confronting her husband in the hope he would admit it. Then she could give him hell, make him promise not to see her again and maybe, just maybe, they might be able to salvage their marriage.

But Paul Birch was ruining those plans for his wife. After a few years as an astute local politician, he knew that he should never confess unless confronted by incontrovertible evidence. And his hot-tempered wife was going purely on a hunch. It would take more than that to make him tell all.

He did not see the bottle smashing down on the back of his head until it was too late. But Paul Birch certainly felt the searing pain as some splinters of glass embedded themselves in his balding pate. Julie Birch was incensed. This was the ultimate insult. She knew he was seeing someone else but he would not admit it. Now she feared that his affair might develop into something even more long-term. The thought of losing him made Julie even more enraged. She was like a cheetah with a short fuse, ready to strike out at any moment — and that moment had just come.

Paul Birch tried very hard to contain himself in the

31

seconds after his wife's attack. He did not want to respond. He was a master at self-control and now he was facing the ultimate test.

Calmly he got up, walked into the bathroom and started removing the splinters of glass embedded in his skull. Meanwhile in the hallway outside, she continued a tirade of abuse that was heard at the other end of the street. Those "good, quiet" neighbours the Birches had suddenly and violently erupted into a couple with problems.

A few minutes later, Paul Birch packed a suitcase in silence as his sobbing wife begged forgiveness and, without a word, walked out of her life, he hoped, for ever. It seemed the best course to take. He knew Julie would only get more and more possessive, and he was also concerned about that temper of hers. Its tendency to explode for no good reason was of very great concern to him. But then she considered she had every right to feel angry, and a lot of wives would probably agree.

To say Julie Birch was heartbroken about the break-up of her marriage to Paul would be an understatement. She was devastated. She could not concentrate at work. The flat was in a constant state of chaos. Her whole life revolved around thinking about him every waking minute of the day. Her sense of betrayal was overwhelming. It was as if her whole world had just crashed into nothing. Without Paul, there was no reason to work. No reason to cook. No reason to make love. No reason to live.

She was 45 years old. Her husband had left her. Her kids did not live with her. Julie Birch felt more than just washed up. She was convincing herself that the whole disaster was all her fault. Maybe she had been too possessive? Perhaps she should have handled things differently? But the bottom line was that she was a passionate woman who could not change her ways. She had always been a very upfront, honest sort of person and it was too late to change.

The trouble was that she believed she had brought it all on herself. It was the classic scenario. He had done wrong. He had gone off with another woman. But now, in the cold light of day, she was blaming herself.

Quite simply, the torment was killing her spirit and her appetite for life — and when that happens people start to get desperate.

"Bastard. I'm gonna pour acid over both of you in the street."

It was a short, sharp message delivered with the hatred that only a scorned woman can muster. The first few threats seemed harmless enough to Paul Birch and his new lover. But, at the back of his mind he kept remembering the things his wife used to say during their time together.

"I'll blast your balls to bits."

It sent a shiver up his spine. But he tried to push those worrying thoughts into the background as he attempted to get on with his new relationship.

If only he had known that Julie Birch had already bought herself a dress... to be buried in after she committed the ultimate sacrifice in the name of wedded bliss. If only he had known that she had made out a will specifically to cover the event of her death in violent circumstances. If only he had known just how distraught she had really become.

Julie Birch counted out the money in ten crisp twenty-pound notes before she exchanged pleasantries with the man who sat next to her in a car parked near one of the roughest council estates in Kingston.

Naturally, he re-counted the cash before handing over her purchase — a sawn-off shotgun of the type preferred by Essex-based bank robbers rather than by your everyday jealous wives.

But her underworld contact asked no questions. As

33

far as he was concerned, it was none of his business what she intended to do with that lethal weapon.

Julie Birch wrapped the gun in a piece of cloth and put it in a holdall before getting out of the man's car and heading back to her job at the hairdressing salon. She didn't feel in the least bit bad about what she was about to do. On the contrary, she was already starting to feel relief. Paul would get his just desserts.

Rush-hour on the afternoon of July 16, 1987, seemed a fairly ordinary event in Kingston. It was a reasonably hot summer's day and lots of people were out in the town centre in their shirtsleeves, heading home after a hard day at work.

Amongst those commuters was Julie Birch. She had just left the hairdresser's, carrying that same holdall she used to purchase the sawn-off shotgun two days previously. But now that bag contained another item as well: her burial dress.

Julie was excited in a nervous sort of way. At last the big day had come. She had phoned Paul earlier and convinced him to come to the flat in Horace Road to "discuss a few things". Paul had been relieved that she sounded so composed, so calm. He had been very worried about her response to him ever since she smashed that bottle over his head a few months earlier. Now perhaps they could discuss in a civilised manner the details about their divorce arrangements. But divorce was the last thing on Julie Birch's mind.

Paul Birch felt a little strange having to knock on the door of his own flat when he turned up just after five that afternoon. After many years of walking the short route to and from work, he had to admit he missed the convenience of living so near to his job. But that was just one of the sacrifices he had made in the name of love.

As his wife opened the door to him, he stood there

for a moment, awkward about what to do next. A kiss or similar greeting seemed out of the question when he looked at Julie's face. He could see the tension in her eyes. The feeling of betrayal was clearly lingering within her. He tried to be polite but it was hard to ignore her agitated state. He just prayed that she wouldn't start smashing bottles over his head again.

"Bastard."

This time Paul Birch could not fail to see it coming. She had whipped out the sawn-off shotgun more like a Basildon bank robber than a quietly spoken 45-year-old mother of three. Julie Birch knew exactly where to aim. She was going to make sure that if she could not have him, then no-one else ever would again.

Julie held the stump-like weapon at an angle, with the squat double barrels aimed downwards at his groin, and pulled the trigger without a moment's hesitation. The pellets connected with his thigh, just inches from the spot that his wife was really trying to hit.

"No. No. No. Oh my God."

The Birches neighbours had heard them argue many times over the previous few months but when they heard those gun shots even they realised there was something definitely more serious happening this time. The net curtains at the bay windows of all those houses must have been working overtime as resident after resident came to their window to see what those shots were all about.

Inside the flat, the carnage had only just begun...

Julie Birch was disappointed by her aim. The intention had been to blast his balls to bits. She had always kept her word. It was the least he deserved. But she wanted to keep the other cartridge for herself. So now, she would have to use a different method to teach him never to cheat on her again.

She pulled out a knife and looked down at the moaning figure in the living room of that once-cosy

35

lovenest where they had shared so many passionate moments. He was looking up at her. His eyes pleading for mercy. In his thigh a bloody wound. But it wasn't enough. And as Paul Birch looked at his wife he must have sensed the horrors that were about to follow.

Julie hitched up her skirt and straddled her husband just the way she had straddled him all those years before when she had taught him so much about making love. But this time her intention was not to have sex with him.

For a few moments she glared down at him. A twisted smirk on her face. She was enjoying his obvious agony. Now it was time to cause some more.

The first time she sank the blade into his chest, she felt the ripping of his flesh as bone hit handle. Her husband gasped for air beneath her, hyperventilating like some desperate asthma sufferer. Julie stopped for a split second — in a weird way it was not that dissimilar from what happened when they had sex together. But his stomach and groin area was where she was aiming her knife. The second plunge of that deadly weapon proved even more lethal. His gut was now ripped open like a plastic bin liner that had been overfilled. His organs were squelching and seeping out through the thin layer of fat.

As four policemen tried to break down the front door to the flat, she inflicted at least three more deadly wounds to the crimson mess of what was once her vibrant, healthy husband.

And when the officers actually managed to burst in, she turned the shotgun on herself as she sat there still straddling her husband in a bizarre, sexually provocative pose — and fired into her heart. Unfortunately, she missed her target that time as well and ended up shooting herself in the shoulder.

The four policemen were astounded by what they found. The bloody, but still just alive, Paul Birch was writhing in agony under the full weight of his shapely, blood-splattered wife. Four and a half hours later,

Paul Birch died in Kingston Hospital. Doctors said he bled to death after his wife had punctured his heart during the frenzied knife attack.

In August, 1988, Julie Beulah Birch was committed to a mental hospital for an indefinite period after she admitted the manslaughter of her husband on the grounds of diminished responsibility.

During the trial at Southwark Crown Court, defending counsel Mrs Nemone Lethbridge said: "She really cannot remember anything after the shot. She had a brainstorm. It was a rotten marriage."

In a taped interview Julie Birch said: "I had planned it for some time. Killing Paul to me is like getting rid of a slug. It was the greatest pleasure I have had in my entire life — pulling the trigger."

The following year, three appeal court judges overruled the Southwark Crown Court judge who sentenced Birch, saying that the doctors at the hospital where she was held — who did not feel she was a general danger to the public — could decide when she was well enough to be released. Today, she is believed to be a free woman.

3

Under The Willow Tree

"What's this shit?"

Tom Scotland had a way with words which few people appreciated, least of all his good wife June. His favourite response at meal times was to throw the remains of his food right at her if it did not meet his approval.

And on that particular day in the summer of 1987, he was keeping to his own traditional behaviour pattern yet again. This time it was the meat pie that induced the Tom Scotland pig-of-the-month performance.

"Call this food? A leper wouldn't touch it, you useless piece of shit."

Twenty years. She'd put up with it since the beginning. Sometimes she wondered why. But then she remembered the kids. Someone had to look after them, bring them up in the world and teach them the basics. And Tom Scotland wasn't much of a father, so it was all left to June.

As she removed the bits of pie crust and splodgy gravy from her housecoat, she really did wonder if it was all worth it. She looked down at him sitting smugly there at the dinner table stamping his feet, and let the loathing build up.

How dare he treat her like that? What right had he to shout and abuse her? Other women would have left long ago. Even her relatives had tried to persuade her. Just walk out on him. But for the children... She had to protect them. She had no job, no independent income. June Scotland was trapped, but she was finally coming to the conclusion that it was time to start planning her escape.

As she stood there in the kitchen of their modest three-bedroomed house in Stevenage, she felt a new, hardened anger flood through her. But June was quickly snapped out of those thoughts when Scotland came charging towards the fridge.

Before she could utter a word, he ripped it open and started grappling through the contents like some desperate beggar on the streets of Calcutta. Soon the contents were spread all over the kitchen floor and her husband was cursing them just as much as he cursed June at the dinner table.

"What's this?" He threw a dish of stew she had lovingly prepared into the air. The brown gravy splattered across the floor she had spent so much time making pristinely clean just a few hours earlier.

"And this?" He pulled out a plate load of uncooked hamburgers and ground them into the cracks between the tiles with the heel of his work boots.

"Why can't you ever make me the sort of food I like? Not this rubbish."

June was heartbroken. It had happened before. But this time it was really hitting her hard. She wondered how she had managed to endure all those years of insults. He had no right treating her this way. But what could she do? In reality, there was only one answer. That day marked the start of the countdown to Tom Scotland's death.

"But do they work?"

June Scotland was most concerned about whether the travel sickness tablets she was about to purchase at her local chemist really were effective.

When she asked about obvious precautions like not taking them together with sleeping pills, the shop assistant must have thought she was a pretty sensible lady simply preparing for a holiday in some sunshine location. For the residents of Stevenage, Spain was probably the most popular place to go, although June had no intention of even getting on an aeroplane, let alone spending any time away from her tidy little house in Pankhurst Crescent.

As she walked back home through the quiet, neat streets, she could feel a real buzz of excitement from within. It was almost as if she were going on a holiday. She was so looking forward to this time next week. She would be free for the first time in twenty-two years. No more emotional torture. No more pain and suffering. No more sleepless nights filled with the fear of what tomorrow holds. But, most important of all, there would be no more opportunities for that animal to get his hands on their daughter.

That was what hurt June the most. Less than four years earlier her pretty dark-haired daughter had come home from school one day looking like death. Her face was pale. Her eyes were watery. She was shaking with fear. Caroline Scotland was just 15 years old and the truth had just dawned on her that her father — her own flesh and blood, the man who had helped bring her into the world — had been forcing her to have sex with him.

At first, he'd touched her and stroked her in places that did not seem natural. That was when she was just 11 years old. He would catch her in the garden and carry her into the shed, where he would sit her down and start to let his fingers run lines across her soft, young skin. She did not even realise what he was doing at first. Something told her that it was not right. But she was afraid to tell anyone, even her mum. It seemed better just to let things be. She did not want to start yet another fight between her parents. She had seen enough of the rows to last a lifetime. She did not want to be the cause of more.

But then it got more serious. Scotland was not content with gratifying his sick sexual demands through touching and feeling. He wanted more. By the time Caroline had reached her teens she was no longer a virgin. Her innocence had been bruised and destroyed by that animal who called himself her father. For two years, he carried on thrusting his perverted demands on his daughter. He preyed on her innermost fears. He threatened her with awful consequences if she so much as mentioned a word of it to her mother.

Basically, she was suppressing the truth from herself, as is often the case with victims of incest. He would do the act. She would go back to sleep. The next day, those dreadful memories would be locked out of her mind, hidden away in a fragment of her brain that would keep them safe until something sparked them off again.

For at least two years that part of her mind absorbed the sexual abuse and then tucked it away out of sight. It was only when she began talking with her friends at school about sex that she realised with a shocking force that what he did to her was completely and utterly wrong. And the picture came back together...

At first, they were just quick flashes. A hand on her knee. Her dress buttons being unfastened. The flare of his hairy nostrils as he leaned close to her lips. After that, the dam burst and she relived the experiences with sickening clarity. Finally, she could take no more and decided to tell her mum.

Like any caring mother, June was horrified. The man she had once loved and cherished had forced their innocent little daughter to have sex with him. The two of them just wept in each other's arms.

Caroline tried to take her own life. It was June's most terrifying experience. Walking in on her as she was in the process of attempting to kill herself. Luckily, June prevented the tragedy, but she could do nothing to stop Caroline's nightmares. Like the time her father took her favourite teddy bear and threw it in the blazing fireplace just because she had written on the wall. He did not spare his two sons either. They nicknamed him "Mr Killjoy". But it turned out to be a tragic underestimate of his real intentions towards his family.

The two days following her purchase of those travel sickness pills were filled with anguish for June Scotland.

41

The plan to end her marriage to a monster was underway, but she wondered if she really would have the courage to see it through. She kept playing with that tiny bottle of tablets in her handbag every time she thought about what to do. But she simply could not get herself to take them out and make the inevitable happen.

Each night, when he came home from his job as an electrician, she found herself thrown back into his awful, abusive world. The insults were continuous. It was like the worst kind of mental torture and, yet, what made it even more painful was the knowledge that she now had the power to end his life. All she had to do was unscrew that bottle and pour the pills into his food. It was that easy.

But it wasn't until the third morning — on August 25, 1987 — that June made the fateful decision that would alter the course of her entire life.

As usual, she woke up early to prepare the breakfast that her bullying husband always expected. She turned to face him in the bed. When he actually slept, it was the only time he looked vaguely pleasant. But beneath those closed eyelids, she knew the monster was still very much alive — and in just a few minutes the inevitable torture would begin all over again.

June Scotland had decided. She lay there in the bed next to him and thought: "Yes, today is the day I'm going to kill you." That was it. She had promised herself it would happen. Not just for her. For the sake of Caroline. For the sake of a peaceful, happy life.

"Hey! What's all this? We celebratin' something?"

Even when his wife prepared his favourite meal of stir-fry turkey, Tom Scotland could not sound in the least bit grateful. Most husbands would have grabbed their wife and kissed her in recognition of the special effort. But not Scotland. It was almost as if he preferred coming home to pour scorn and abuse on his family. Happiness did not come easily to Tom Scotland.

He eyed his wife suspiciously across the kitchen. His instincts told him she was up to something. When June turned and faced him, she knew she was doing the right thing. Maybe if he had shown some compassion or loving towards her, then she might have felt a twinge of guilt and perhaps she would have decided to abandon her plan.

But, instead, he was playing right into her hands. His gruff, ungrateful manner was yet more confirmation in her own mind that he was about to get what he deserved.

As usual, the meal was eaten in virtual silence. Caroline was upstairs listening to records in her room. She preferred not to eat in the presence of her father. She could not stand to feel his eyes bearing down on her from the sofa, where he sat glued to the television as he ate. She could not handle the knowledge that he was sitting there having devoured her body in every sense. The very thought that he was so close to her in front of her mother filled Caroline with disgust and loathing. She preferred to be alone with her thoughts. Why should she exchange pleasantries with that animal?

June Scotland sat down opposite her husband in the lounge and watched him eating the stir-fry turkey with a feeling of immense satisfaction. At last the time had come. She examined each mouthful as he scoffed back the food. She thought she could see the white remnants of those forty-odd travel sickness pills in amongst the turkey and vegetables. She hesitated for a moment when he caught her staring straight at his plate. But he said nothing. Tom Scotland had long since given up communicating with his wife. He was not about to change the habit of a lifetime by questioning her actions now.

Any normal, loving husband might have at least complimented June on her culinary skills. Not this husband though. He just carried on pitch-forking the food into his mouth. June watched him and smiled inside. He attacked the dinner as though it were his last...

June was already starting to feel that sense of relief that comes after you have achieved something you so carefully set out to do. She retreated to the kitchen because she could not stand to watch him any longer. Her emotions were torn in two. Here she was, killing the man she had promised to love and adore for the rest of her life. Yet every time she looked at him she knew why it just had to be done.

She peered through the kitchen hatch. He mopped his plate with a piece of bread and let out a contented burp. For once, such a sweet sound. It was a signal. It would not be long now...

Tom Scotland was not feeling at all well. Within minutes of finishing that last mouthful of his favourite meal, he tried to get up to go to the toilet and almost fell flat on his face. He closed his eyes for a moment. The image of that food was swimming around inside his head. It made him feel nauseous, so he blinked open his eyes once more. The room was moving. He could hardly focus on his beloved TV set, let alone make out what show was on.

He tried again to get to his feet. This time he just made it by holding onto the arm of the sofa, but it was a real struggle. One step at a time, he tried to move toward the door. He nearly fell over a chair and just regained his balance.

By the time Tom Scotland got to the hallway from the living room, he felt as if he'd just walked a hundred miles. From the kitchen, June watched him without uttering a word. One half of her felt like helping him but the other, more realistic half, stopped her. She could not, and would not, save him. This was all meant to be.

Heavy rock music blared out from his daughter's room. He wished she would turn the bloody thing off, but he hadn't the strength to shout. When Tom Scotland caught a glimpse of his wife watching him calmly from the kitchen, it dawned on him for the first time that she had just sentenced him to death. Even through his swirling thoughts, he could see it in her eyes. This time, it was her turn to show no emotion. Her hands were folded tersely in front of her. He knew.

"Get the doctor."

He could barely utter the words. And when he did, it felt as if someone else was saying them. But June did not move towards him as he half collapsed there on the floor. She did not say a word as he crawled, like some wounded soldier, slowly up the stairs towards his bedroom.

Instead, she quietly pulled open the nearest drawer in the kitchen and took out a rolling pin. The very object that is so often used to illustrate a wife's anger with her husband was now about to become the ultimate weapon.

By the time she got to the stairs, he had already managed to crawl through the bedroom door. She knew she had to be quick, otherwise he might get to the telephone.

The first blow of that rolling pin smashed into the side of his head as he crawled towards the sanctuary of his bed. Incredibly, it helped rather than hindered Scotland's fight for life. Somehow, the blow to his head helped clear his mind momentarily. His vision straightened out significantly and any doubts about his wife's intentions had been wiped from his mind.

He grabbed hold of the rolling pin and tried to yank it out of his wife's grasp. They grappled like two sumo wrestlers on the floor of the bedroom. She managed to hold onto her weapon of destruction though.

Then Tom Scotland tried to make for the door as another blow rained past his head, missing him by inches. It was his only chance. He had to get out of that room.

The heavy rock music was still blaring out from Caroline's room, drowning out the sound of the deadly attack that was about to reach a crescendo.

But June was not going to let him get away. She pursued him onto the landing outside the bedrooms. It was a small floorspace and, as the husband and wife continued their life-and-death struggle, they fell down the stairs. Rolling like stuntmen out of a cops-and-robbers film, they seemed to keep falling in slow motion as the angle of the stairway slowed their descent.

June was the first one to get up when they landed at the foot of the stairs. She still had that rolling pin grasped in her hand. A look of steely determination on her face. For a moment she looked down at the pathetic mess of a man who once claimed he loved her. Then he stirred and tried to get back on his feet. By moving, he simply encouraged the killer instinct within June to rear up again. To finish off the job she had set out to do.

The last blow went crashing through his skull with all the strength she could summon. The blood from the wound splattered everywhere in the hallway as the noise of Caroline's heavy metal record reached its own musical crescendo at exactly the same moment. Bits of gristle splattered the floor and walls. That last crunching blow literally crushed his brain to bits.

June stood there for a moment taking in the scene. It all seemed so unreal. Had she really just done all that to her husband? For a few minutes she could not absorb the reality of the situation. It was as if she were completely detached from it. Only when her daughter Caroline appeared beside her did it really all dawn on her.

Caroline was 18 years old, but those memories of her father's illicit sexual intercourse with her were as fresh as yesterday in her mind. That's why she showed no emotion as she looked down at his twisted, pathetic

46

body lying there in a crumpled heap on the floor.

With her mother standing beside her, she stared into his matt, glazed eyes. There was no flicker of life left in them. Nothing. But still they had a strange hypnotic effect on her. It was as if the devil inside him was waiting to leap out at her and drag her into the bedroom for yet more sexual abuse.

She checked for pulses in the neck and wrist — there was nothing. Her mother watched her admiringly. Amazed that her little baby could be so professional. So calm. So cool. So collected. But there were other thoughts running through Caroline's mind. She could not keep her eyes off him. Her gaze kept being drawn to his face. The mask of death.

"Even when he was dead he looked evil," said Caroline later.

She leant down and closed his eyelids firmly. It was a remarkable attempt to seek reassurance that the monster had finally departed from that terrified household.

"It was like she hadn't killed him, that he was alive. He looked evil and I had to shut them."

Mother and daughter exchanged few words. The shock of witnessing the end of their torment spoke louder than any words. Caroline decided she had to take control of the situation. Her mother was shaking with fear. She had done it, but now she was terrified of the consequences. Her teenage daughter — always incredibly close to June — was about to show maturity well beyond her age. She was going to grow up right before her mother's very eyes.

The bottle of Bacardi was shaking as June Scotland poured it into two tumblers for her and her daughter. They sat on the same sofa where only a few minutes earlier Tom Scotland had devoured that poisoned feast which marked the start of his journey to death.

The door to the living room was shut. They did

47

not want to be able to see the bloody remains of Tom Scotland as they discussed what to do next. There was little doubt in Caroline's mind — she was not going to let the man who abused and terrorised her drag them both into the arms of the law. She was convinced that there was a way to avoid all that.

Two stiff Bacardis later they had agreed a plan. June's oldest son Alan had long since moved out of home and her other son Alistair was away. The house was empty except for the two of them. They had time on their side.

Caroline dropped a sheet over the bloody remains of her father so that it covered him from head to toe. No hint of his bluing, pallid skin was exposed. The last thing either of them wanted was to have to see him there whenever they walked through the hallway.

June was about to go into her bedroom — the same room she had shared with the monster — when she remembered the bloody evidence of her first crushing blow to his head was spread around the carpet. It was too much. She could not bear to go in there. She stopped Caroline on the landing and persuaded her to sleep with her in young Alistair's room. It was the only place in that tiny, modest house where there were no actual reminders of the killing that had just occurred.

Neither June nor Caroline had a particularly good night's sleep. Their waking moments were filled with the living nightmare they had just endured. Their dreams were filled with even more graphic, outrageous images brought on by the real-life horrors they had just been involved in.

The early dawn light had only just started peeping through the curtains in Alistair's bedroom when the two women decided they had to get up to complete their grisly task.

48

"Come on. Let's just get on with it."

Caroline was now firmly in charge. She was paying him back for all that abuse. She could not stand the thought of her mother paying the penalty for something she wished she'd done herself.

Armed with mops, clothes, rubber gloves and every cleaning implement they could find, the two women began methodically cleaning the house from top to bottom. Spring-cleaning time had come early in the Scotland household.

After hours of fanatical scrubbing, Caroline and June laid their mops on the floor for a moment and looked down from the landing at the crumpled sheet that covered what was once the brutal, bruising figure of 48-year-old Tom Scotland. They still had not touched the body. It was as if they were subconsciously hoping that by cleaning the house, his body might just magically disappear and they would not have to face the gruesome task of disposing of the corpse.

But he was still there when Caroline clinically lifted the sheet to start the operation to dispose of his body.

They struggled to wrap the body in a plastic sheet. Every time they managed to lift up one end of his stiff, lifeless body they couldn't quite squeeze it under. Finally, after many attempts, they managed to seal Tom Scotland from the outside world for ever. His body looked weirdly distorted through the plastic covering. Luckily, it gave the whole proceedings an unreal aura. His skin had changed colour and he no longer looked like the evil man both women had grown to hate.

"Let's take him to the shed."

Caroline was once again firmly in charge. She lifted him from the heavier end as her mum struggled to hold his legs. Caroline was thankful that she had closed his eyelids the previous night. The very thought of him staring coldly at her through the plastic, as

49

they half dragged him through the pitch black that next evening, would have probably scared her to death.

As it was, both women had somehow mentally detached themselves from the task at hand — and things were by no means over yet.

After dumping his rotting corpse on the muddy floor of the garden shed, Caroline looked around herself for a moment and remembered those horrific times just a few years earlier when he would take her in that very same shed and touch her and hurt her.

It must have given her the strangest feeling of satisfaction to know that she had voluntarily walked back into that shed now — with his lifeless body completely under her control this time. There was absolutely nothing he could do to prevent her from getting revenge for all those appalling attacks.

It wasn't until the following evening that June and Caroline finally got rid of him. Once again, it was the daughter who came to the rescue.

As June sat shaking with nerves in the kitchen, Caroline grabbed hold of her father's favourite spade and started digging his grave for him.

It took four hours to get the hole big enough. Caroline was completely exhausted. She had no idea it would be so difficult when she set out to dig the grave. It wasn't helped by the fact that she had to do it all in complete silence for fear that one of the nosy neighbours of Pankhurst Crescent might hear something suspicious and call the police.

But at least she had picked a spot just beneath his favourite (and only) weeping willow tree. He did not deserve any sympathy, but it seemed only right to lie him to rest amongst the rotting roots of that vast tree which had dominated Caroline's view from her bedroom window for most of her life.

Back in the kitchen, June was nervously sipping at

her favourite drink, Bacardi. She was dreading the next stage in their plan — the lowering of the body. She kept having nightmarish thoughts about him still being alive. Breaking free of that plastic covering and killing them all in an act of bitter-sweet revenge. She really did not want to go out there on that warm August night and even so much as see the shape of his corpse through the plastic.

"Come on, mum. The quicker we do it, the better."

Caroline was almost business-like about it all, but she was merely stifling her emotions so as not to make things any worse for her mother. That was her priority all along — her mum. Yet, she herself had a lot to gain by getting rid of him for ever. Her life might actually start to be worth living again. Perhaps those suicidal feelings would go away for ever. It was worth getting rid of him for that alone.

"I can't go through with this — I want to end it now and tell someone."

June had broken down in tears. The prospect of burying her own husband was too much. Caroline had to think quick. This was not the way it was meant to be.

"No one will understand why you did it. We've got to do it this way."

June took another almighty swig of Bacardi, held her head up high and walked single-mindedly out to the end of the garden, just beneath the weeping willow.

The thud that sounded as his body crashed into the shallow grave just beneath the weeping willow tree was muted. It did not echo.

"I'm sorry."

Caroline looked in astonishment at her mother. She was apologising to the monster who had so nearly ruined all their lives.

The sound of the earth being sprinkled over the plastic sheeting was quite distinct at first. Each shovel-load landed with a definite noise.

"I'm sorry."

She said those words again. Caroline tried to understand why her mother should feel any sorrow for that man, but she could not truly appreciate it.

It was only after his entire body had been completely covered by its first layer of earth that the noise became more muffled and insignificant. It was also then that June Scotland stopped saying sorry to her husband.

"He's gone to work in Saudi Arabia. Won't be back for years."

It seemed the perfect excuse for Tom Scotland's absence. Some concerned neighbours replied: "That's a long time. Won't you miss him?" But June Scotland ignored those remarks and just got on with her life.

For three and a half years no-one questioned her or her family about his departure. It was as if most people were glad to see the back of him; otherwise, perhaps they would have cared a little more.

June was just relieved to have a life to live once more. She loved staying at home and looking after the baby Caroline had had a year or so after her father's death. Often they'd both sit at the kitchen table and look out at that stretch of grass at the end of the garden and think about him. But it was always merely a passing thought. There was no regret. They knew it had had to be done. They shared the ultimate secret but they never once felt tempted to tell anyone else. Their mother–daughter relationship was strangely bonded even more closely by the events that had occurred. It was as if they were both just grateful for the chance to live again.

Neither Caroline nor June seemed unduly worried when their houseproud neighbour Ted Bunce decided to erect a new, pristine garden fence just near the weeping willow.

As Ted dug a series of small holes in the ground to make the fence more stable, he could not possibly

52

have known what lay just under his feet — until he spotted the plastic sheet coming through the soil. And through that cover he noticed a hand. He stopped digging immediately.

June Scotland felt numb as she looked through her living room window to see police cordoning off the back garden. Suddenly the full realisation of what had happened three and half years earlier dawned on her. She knew full well why they were there. In her heart of hearts she had known this day would eventually come, despite her daughter's sterling efforts to cover up the death of Tom Scotland.

With tears streaming down her face, she ran through the house. But this was no desperate attempt to escape. She knew she had to do one thing before they called at her door and arrested her.

She knocked desperately on the door of her son Alistair's room. He was stunned when she said to him: "I've got something to tell you."

"Is it granny or grandad?" asked Alistair, sensing the impending doom in her voice.

"No. Worse. They've found your father in the garden. I hit him with a rolling pin."

Alistair hugged his mother tightly and they just stood there for a few seconds in silence. Then there was a knock at the door.

June Scotland took a deep breath, went downstairs and calmly let the police in.

In March 1992, June Scotland, aged 52, was sentenced to two years' probation after being convicted at Luton Crown Court of manslaughter on the grounds of diminished responsibility. A jury cleared her of the greater charge of murder after Judge Justice Garland said:

"No good whatsoever would be served by seeking to punish you further."

Her daughter Caroline received two years' probation

53

after admitting preventing a lawful burial. Justice Garland told her:

"When you were 18 you found yourself in a situation that must have been impossible, almost an intolerable burden on you."

June Scotland has now changed her surname by deed poll after announcing: "The name of Scotland is too unusual. We plan to move somewhere and start a new life."

Tragically, she is estranged from both her sons following her arrest for the murder of their father.

4

Fifth Time Lucky

As they kissed each other fully on the lips, she pushed her tongue deep into his mouth. She felt his hands pulling at her breasts through her tight-fitting silk blouse. His forefinger and thumb tweaked expertly at her acorn-shaped nipples peeping through the cream-coloured lace bra. This was how it should be. It felt right now. She was glad she had waited. It made the night special. Six hours ago she had said 'I will'. And now she was.

They fell back onto the hotel waterbed. It quivered in response, accommodated their movements. They lay there, locked together in a passionate embrace, while the water rippled underneath them. She was starting to relax with a man for the first time in her life. She had always promised herself that she would not do it until she had found the perfect partner. Now that dream was coming true — and it was proving to be just as amazing as she had hoped for.

She grabbed him gently between the legs and squeezed. He winced slightly at first. Surprised, she pulled her hand away. But he enjoyed a little pain with the pleasure. It turned him on. He pushed her hand back down there and smiled at her. It was a look of reassurance. Go on, it said, *do it*!

The throbbing was so strange. It seemed to have a will of its own, a little animal with its own personality. She rested her head against his chest and realised with a giggle that it pulsed in time with his heartbeat. She wondered how the afterwaves of the heart could travel so far down. She stroked him and coaxed him, urging it to swell even more. Now that her hand had got used to the feel of the silky flesh, she wanted to tease the tip with the base of her thumb. Just to see what would happen. So she pinched it, just as he had faintly tweaked her nipples only a few moments earlier.

This time his wince became a moan of pleasure. It was music to her ears. For the first time in her life she was in control, making her man writhe in ecstasy with just a simple touch.

She knew she could do it with him... She could not wait to feel him inside her. Lovingly. Knowingly. Sensitively.

Until that evening they had come very close to having sex but she had refused to go all the way until they were married. Now, he had allowed her to lead and she was giving him more pleasure than he had ever thought possible.

Often in the past, he had sought out the services of local prostitutes because of her refusal. He convinced himself that he was doing her a favour by going with the street walkers, because it stopped him from feeling the urge to ravish her despite her protests.

Paying for sex had been rather satisfying because it required no effort. He found something exciting about the transaction. Often, he would leave her at her mother's house, having got no more than a lingering kiss on the doorstep. That had been enough to ignite the flames of passion inside him but certainly not sufficient to satisfy his urges. Within minutes, he would be kerb-crawling in the nearby red-light district looking for a suitable sexual partner. He felt no guilt about having sex with prostitutes. They provided a service which he was more than happy to take advantage of.

Most of the girls were gaudily dressed, humourless people who saw their job as a form of torture that had to be endured because it helped pay the rent, subsidised their drug habit, and, if there was any left over, helped out with the cost of clothing their kids.

He had a particular favourite who was not like the rest. She must have been at least 40 years old. But her long, dark, flowing hair hid those giveaway lines. He found her attractive the first time he saw her, and tried desperately to find her each time he came looking for sexual favours.

But it was not just her looks that he found so satisfying. She had an experienced eye. She had been a street walker for more than twenty years and she spoke in the sort of philosophical terms that you would never expect from a lady of the night. She sussed him out the first time they met.

"Don't tell me. Your girlfriend won't do it until you're married."

He nodded his head, smiling to himself at her ability to gauge him so quickly.

She never made him feel dirty or guilty and she liked to talk and laugh. It was that sense of humour that distinguished her from the rest. And there was a hidden bonus. Over the months he went to her, she began to teach him things about sex that he never knew existed. In a weird way, it helped him prepare for that first night with the girl he had just married...

The heat in that hotel bedroom was intense. It seemed to drip from the walls, and the air hung close around their skin like a blanket. Sweat covered their bodies, providing a natural massage oil for their caresses. He loved the way his hand slid across her breasts. She adored feeling the stickiness of his hairy thighs as she stroked a triangle around his groin.

The more foreplay they engaged in, the more she found her enjoyment increasing. She just had no idea it would be as good as this.

The months of apprehension about this night had long since vanished with his first touch. In their place was a floating sensation. She wanted it to go on and on for ever. She knew that eventually one spark would be enough to send her into a climax. But for the moment she still had a lot more to do. She prayed that he would not enter her yet. She wanted it so much, but at the same wanted the anticipation to last for ever. There was so much more to be done.

The sheets on the waterbed had long since come

off in the heat of their passion. Their slippery bodies glistened in the neon light of the flashing hotel sign just outside their window. Each movement was registered by the noise of the rush of water in the bed underneath them.

She kept fighting the urge to have him inside her because she wanted to experience so many other pleasures first. She licked her hand with her tongue, used her moistened fingers to tantalise him even further. He smiled to himself for a split second — it was exactly the same thing that his favourite prostitute used to do to him every time they met. Just thinking about that other woman increased his sexual frenzy even further. As her hand worked up and down on him, he felt himself getting close to coming. He was desperate not to climax yet because he knew he had to save that for the ultimate act but, on the other hand, this felt just as enjoyable.

He grabbed her wrist in an attempt to stop her pumping hand. But she carried on relentlessly pushing and pulling, aware of the outrageous pleasure she was inciting. Then he squeezed her wrist really tightly and she pulled her hand away in pain.

"That hurt."

He did not reply, but smiled back at her and spread her legs apart before mounting her. He needed to do it before it was too late. She lay there, rigid with an unbelievable stab of pain as he forced himself into her. A tear rolled down her cheek. She had a strange feeling about him for the first time in her life. He hadn't reacted when he hurt her then. In fact, his smile had widened into an evil-looking lear.

The warm feeling had gone. This was not how it was meant to be. Her faking as he grunted into her neck. She looked through the window at the flashing sign and wondered why he was making absolutely no effort to kiss her on the lips...

Those first few months of marriage were fairly

uneventful for Jean-Louis and Patricia Orionno. He worked hard during the day at his job in the bank and she kept their flat in the pretty French town of Doubs immaculately clean for when he got home each evening.

Patricia did not really know what to expect from marriage. She often used to think back to that first night of their honeymoon and wonder if she had somewhat over-reacted to his one small sign of brutality towards her. She worried about it because ever since that incident, she had never come anywhere near an orgasm during relentless nights of sex with Jean-Louis.

She tried to talk to her mother about it one morning round at her house, but the only thing she could ascertain was that most men were lusty animals who expected sex whenever and wherever they wanted it. The women were the victims who simply had to open their legs and obey their master's every whim.

Patricia was somewhat shocked by her mother's opinion. It made married life sound so depressing. Why on earth hadn't she told her daughter all this before she walked up the aisle?

"Well. You have to get married, don't you?"

It was, as the French say, a *fait accompli*. But that was not good enough for Patricia. She wanted more than just a servant–master relationship from her marriage. She also wanted to learn how to enjoy sex, rather than feeling as if she were being hit by a battering ram each time he lunged on top of her.

The trouble was that Jean-Louis was only concerned with his own satisfaction. Sure, he had tried to excite her in many varied ways, but she always felt as if he was just doing it for the sake of it. It was as if he felt obliged to make her feel a little excited before the actual act of sex.

One night, Patricia tried to stop Jean-Louis just jumping on top of her and he got very angry.

"Why are you stopping me? I have a right. You are my wife."

And in those words lay the root of all her problems.

59

He thought of sex as something his wife should never refuse. If she did not want it, then she was expected to just lie there and at least pretend to enjoy it so that he could get his own dose of satisfaction.

But poor Patricia had not even had the pleasure of a full, uninhibited orgasm. She was fed up with reading all about the wonders of sex in women's magazines. She wanted them for herself.

Here they were: an attractive couple in their twenties and seemingly so in love. But beneath that veneer of happiness lay a frustration with life so deep that it was tearing Patricia apart. And, to make matters worse, she had no-one to off-load her worries onto. A little bit of talking can go a long way.

Instead, she bottled up her anger and bitterness. It was a vicious circle. Soon she would lose all the vitality and charm that had made her so attractive to Jean-Louis in the first place.

He was working so hard at his job at the local bank, that he did not even notice his wife's change of attitude. Jean-Louis was content just so long as he ate good food, drank good wine and enjoyed regular flurries of sex.

His idea of a dream evening was to walk in from work, smother his wife with kisses, lift up her skirt and take her there and then on the kitchen table. That would be followed by a wonderful four-course meal washed down with a subtle, light red wine and maybe a cognac to round things off. Then, of course, he would retire to the bedroom, where he would breathe a disgusting mix of garlic and alcohol fumes all over his attractive wife as he crushed her under the full weight of his body.

Needless to say, Patricia got more satisfaction out of seeing him enjoying her cooking than through any of his demands in the bedroom. And things were going to get a lot worse.

As the months of marriage turned into years, the couple's inability to produce any offspring simply prompted Jean-Louis to increase his sexual appetite. It was as if he were trying to prove his masculinity by forcing himself on her every single night.

But it was not just a ten-minute grope in bed that he was expecting. As he stepped up his demand for more sex, he did what many husbands do and began trying to make his wife 'experiment'.

Patricia wasn't consulted about whether she was prepared to be handcuffed to their four-poster bed and whipped. Jean-Louis just forced her down on the mattress one night and, gripping her wrists just like he did on their honeymoon, spread her arms and legs wide apart and attached the handcuffs to the bedposts.

As she lay face down on the bed, she was thankful for only one thing. She did not have to see his drunken, glazed eyes feasting on her as he whipped and abused her body. She wished longingly for mere sexual frustration. He had turned into another person, someone she did not recognise, and with it her niggling worries had turned into a nightmare of bestial torture.

Patricia still had no-one to pour her feelings out to. If only she'd had one good friend, then the mounting anger and bitterness might not have reached such a dangerous peak. She was living on the edge. Each time he came near her she shuddered. But she had to let him do whatever he wanted because she was afraid of being punished really severely and, even worse, losing the home she had spent so much time and energy creating.

What hurt her the most was the emotional torture. The physical pain was unbearable, but the knowledge that her own husband did not care how much he abused her crucified her. His idea of sexual contentment was to damage her body and force her to degrade herself through sick and perverted acts. She became worthless. A slab of meat to be picked at whenever he chose.

Patricia's daytime hours provided a temporary escape from the monster who ruled her life with a rod of iron. But his menacing shadow loomed over her even then. Often, she would cry at the kitchen table, her head sunk into folded arms, unaware that morning had turned to afternoon. But eventually the tears were replaced by a new determination. At first it glowed, tiny and warm inside her. But as the months passed it took hold, caught light and became a raging fire. She couldn't take much more of this. She wouldn't take much more. It would be her turn soon, she decided one day, as she sliced up a side of beef for his lordship's evening meal. She stuck the knife in full-force and twisted. She watched the red juices trickle out as the blade turned.

See how he likes it, she thought. The liquid lay in a pool on the chopping board. Just for a moment she thought it was shaped like a heart.

She crushed the white sleeping tablets into the meat pie. It was a meticulous process. She wanted to make sure there was absolutely no sign of them when he devoured the dish on his return from work that evening. She reckoned that twenty pills would probably be enough but she chucked in a further ten just for good measure.

As Patricia Orionno stirred the thick stew of meat and gravy, she felt a surge of happiness for the first time in months. He had driven her to desperate measures. The previous night he had left her tied to the bed for hours while he whipped her and then performed the most dreadful sexual act she had ever experienced in her entire life. When he was finished doing that, he went on to what he considered to be a perfectly normal bit of love-making. But the love had long since disappeared. In its place was a brutal stabbing sensation that burnt her insides like a red hot poker. He did it for hours and hours. By the time she cried herself to sleep, she was in such pain that she wondered how she would even be able to get up the next morning.

But Jean-Louis had the answer to that problem. As orange shafts of early morning sun poured through the bedroom window, he pushed and prodded her until she stirred. She woke to the gagging sensation of him forcing himself into her mouth. The pain barriers had long since been surpassed by a numb feeling that comes when you just don't care any more.

Back in the kitchen on that cold winter's night in early 1988, Patricia could feel the pain each time she moved. It was a constant reminder of the torture he had inflicted on her. It also proved an inspiration. She would do it. And she would do it in the belief that there was no other choice.

When Jean-Louis arrived home an hour later, she might as well have been invisible. He hardly even acknowledged her presence as he struggled to pull the cork from a bottle of his favourite red wine. For once, Patricia was happy that her husband was being his usual uncaring self. She did not want to have any doubts about her scheme to kill him, and she knew that if he showed her any loving attention then she might start to abandon her plans. That would be a disaster. There was no doubt in her mind that he would eventually destroy her if she did not get him first.

As her bullying pig of a husband tucked into his meat pie, he looked like a man without a care in the world. No doubt he was contemplating some more sick sex later that evening. Patricia watched him consume every mouthful. He had become so selfish he did not even bother to ask why she was not joining him for supper. He did not care, just so long as she gave him what he wanted.

Ten minutes later, her husband wiped his plate clean with a chunk of bread. She was so happy. It would not be long now, surely?

Jean-Louis was a fairly well built sort of fellow.

More solid than rotund. And he had a cast-iron stomach, hardened by years of gobbling down tons of rich food. But Patricia's poisonous pie seemed to have got the better of it.

He sat down on the sofa in their living room and let out a huge yawn.

"Shall we go to bed early tonight?" he said, stretching like an overgrown cat.

Normally, that was the signal for a bout of sexual torture too painful to contemplate. But this time, her husband's request met with a genuine response.

"Good idea. I could do with some kip too."

It was working. He would be unconscious in minutes. And there was an added bonus — she would not have to have sex with him that night. Or any other night, ever again, for that matter.

True to his word, Jean-Louis was snoring away within a few moments of his head hitting the pillow. For the first time in years, Patricia Orionno sat up in bed and read a book. It was a romantic novel. Perhaps a knight in shining armour would come riding into her life after her husband's death.

She watched him sleeping. Once in a while, he would grunt, turn onto his side. *Come on. Die. Come on. Die.* But Jean-Louis looked rather too healthy to be anywhere near his death-bed quite yet.

It was a good novel, but Patricia was rather distracted. She kept looking over to see if her husband had made that final passage to hell. But his snoring proved he most certainly had not. She was furious. He had to be dead. He should be dead. But he was very much alive. Even in his slumber, his face had a huge, broad grin on it. Like a mocking challenge.

Patricia had every intention of rising to it. She got out of the bed and crept towards the kitchen. Her fists were clenched in fury. She ripped open a drawer and took out the sharpest knife she could find. This time it was for keeps.

She walked back into the bedroom and looked down at his irritatingly content face and narrowed her eyes in determination at the task at hand. Then she stopped in her tracks. Should she just stab him over and over or should she slit his wrists gently and quietly without even disturbing him? With any luck he would be sufficiently knocked out by the sleeping pills not to feel a thing. But the force and violence required to stab him might awaken him. She decided to slit his wrists.

Like a master craftsman carving a minute wooden figure, she began sawing at the veins on the inside of his wrists. At first, the knife wouldn't penetrate the blue vessels that ran up his arm. In an attempt to bring them to the surface of his skin, she squeezed and twisted them in a Chinese burn. The wounds she finally managed to inflict were pathetic. Little globules of blood oozed from the gashes. No cascade, no glorious red fountain. Patricia did not realise that the massive dose of sleeping pills had slowed down Jean-Louis's circulation so much that even if she had dissected the man like a surgeon, he would have been highly unlikely to bleed to death.

After ten minutes she gave up. There had to be a better way. Or perhaps she should just stop altogether. It was actually starting to seem more appealing to just divorce the brute. But then she remembered what he had done to her only last night. He deserved everything he got.

Perhaps gas would do the trick. She ran a hose pipe from the kitchen into the bedroom and pointed the end straight into the snoring face of her husband. He did not budge an inch.

As the smell of the gas started to make her feel hazy and faint, she realised that Jean-Louis was still enjoying some sweet dream or other and she was in danger of killing herself in the process. What to do with the stubborn bastard? She stepped back from the bed for a moment and looked down at him sleeping peacefully there, as if he did not have a care in the world. He had no right to survive this onslaught but somehow he was still very much alive, if not exactly kicking.

Each time her murderous intentions failed, she felt a surge of bitterness. She kept reminding herself of that abuse. She could still feel the pain he inflicted on her. He could not be allowed to get away with it.

She reached down and picked up a pillow and held it up above her head. His smug face challenged her to do it. She hated every inch of him. Slowly she knelt over his chest. It must have been the first time in her married life that she had been in the dominant position. And a very fitting time too.

She brought the pillow down over his face and held it there with all her might. He started struggling beneath her. His arms came up, grabbed at her breasts, crawled blindly to her neck. He was hurting her now and her grip on the pillow was weakening. She could not hold it down tight enough.

He was taking control again. Wide awake from his pill-induced slumber, he was fighting back and she just was not strong enough to stop him. She looked over at that same knife she had tried to slit his wrists with a few minutes earlier. It was her only chance.

She just managed to lean over to the bedside table and grab it from the slippery glass surface. For a split second she fumbled with it as his hands pummelled into her face. In another few seconds he would emerge victorious once more, unless she took her chance now.

She plunged that razor-sharp knife right into his chest and felt the blade slice through the skin and tissue like paper. She had to be quick. One wound would not be enough. She had to puncture his body until there were enough outlets to drain the energy — and the blood — from him.

Seven more times she slashed into his torso. Each time she felt his body twitch in pain. It was an amazing sensation after all the agony he had inflicted on her. By the time she pulled that knife out for the eighth time, she realised with a mixture of joy and self-disgust that he was finally dead. His limp body lay beneath her. The pillow still covered half his face. But she could see from the one glassy eye now staring out into oblivion that she had finally achieved what she set out to do.

Now she felt nothing inside. She clambered off his body and gave him one last glance, just to make sure there were no signs of life. She was free. But it was a freedom that would be plagued for ever by that terrible night.

On October 23, 1988, Patricia Orionno was allowed to walk free from a court in her home town of Doubs, after the judge found her not guilty of the murder of her husband Jean-Louis.

He called her actions "justifiable" following years of sexual torment at the hands of her vicious husband.

5

The Seaside Killers

Some people had all the luck.

She was just 21 years of age. Thick, dark hair cascaded over slender shoulders. Pert breasts that were the envy of all her girlfriends. Shapely thighs with just the right degree of curve to attract any red-blooded male's attention. Even her ankles were neat and nicely rounded, especially when she was wearing a pair of two-inch heels. Everyone agreed — Gail had the sort of good looks all girls long for.

Even her upbringing in the respectable Buckinghamshire hamlet of Farnham Common gave her a definite edge on most girls of a similar age. It wasn't that she came from such a wealthy background, but the civilised tone of life in such a peaceful place had definitely rubbed off on her.

"She had a certain magnetism," was how her old school pals used to describe it. Lots of friends tried to persuade her to enter the local beauty pageant. But Gail said she was too shy and modest to exhibit her body like some piece of meat in a market place.

Her friends also said that the beautiful brunette could be pretty cold and cunning when she wanted to get her own way. Gail was without doubt a very determined young woman — and she was on the lookout for the right man to fall in love with. Many of her friends reckoned that was precisely why she decided to go on a Mediterranean cruise at such a young age.

Cruises usually consist of middle-aged or elderly couples, plus a sprinkling of spinsters and widows hopefully pursuing some romantic fantasy or other. Not surprisingly, the stunningly attractive Gail stood out like a sore thumb.

She loved the special attention heaped on her by the lustful crew of predominantly under-35-year-old men. She could feel their eyes watching her every movement as she lay sunbathing on the deck in her revealing bikini. She found it all rather flattering. It was the first time in her rather protected life that she had been exposed to men *en masse*. Just so long as they only looked and did not try to touch, she was perfectly happy to lap up the attention.

Cruise rules regarding crew members romancing passengers are fairly rigid, and none of the randy sailors ever actually tried to put their lustful thoughts about Gail into practice. So when she got talking to a rather pleasant man called Graham Jones in the ship's lounge one day, it seemed only natural to accept his offer of dinner that evening.

Jones was just 23 years old at the time, but his age soon seemed at odds with his experience of life. He had seen the world in every sense of the word. But the moment he clapped eyes on Gail he knew he had to have her.

As they sat opposite each other in the ship's dining room, enjoying the most romantic of candle-lit meals, he found himself lost for words a lot of the time. Quite simply, he was instantly besotted by Gail. He could not stop his mind from working overtime. Unfortunately his means of conversation dried up as a result.

Gail, for her part, was equally fascinated by Graham Jones. He seemed the perfect catch. Only a couple of years older than her, but mature with it. His handsome, rugged features reminded her of her father — and that can often be a crucial thing for an impressionable young woman. There is something solid and reliable about a man who looks like your father.

She did not mind the silences between the mouthfuls of food. She knew there was already something really special between them. It was that unique spark of recognition that can only occur between two strangers destined to be together.

Gail felt his hand reach over and grasp her slender

fingers on that dining room table. She closed her eyes for a moment and felt the tingle of romance flowing through her mind. This was going to be the sort of cruise that dreams are made of. Beautiful flat ocean. Gorgeous sunsets. And, most important of all, a handsome romantic man to take back to Britain.

Ten years later, the memories of that incredible cruise were just a distant flicker in Gail Jones's memory. True, she had married her good-looking cruise-time romeo. And they had started a family. But Graham Jones had gone the way of so many husbands burdened by the pressures of supporting a wife and children. Quite simply, the romance had completely disappeared from their relationship.

Graham was more concerned with providing a good home and enough cash to live a good life. The trouble was that in pursuit of that dream, he had allowed his still-very-pretty wife to become bored and lonely as the family trekked across England while he went from job to job.

He described himself in his CV as a trained time-and-motion engineer. Gail never really understood what that actually meant. But she was sure of one thing — her husband's ability to keep his young family on the move all the time was unquestionable. It was also rather tedious. They never settled long enough in one place for her to make real friends in the neighbourhood where they lived. That often led to long, lonely days at home with the two kids. She couldn't get a job because they were too young to go to school, but she desperately needed something to do with her life. It was a classic dilemma experienced by housewives the world over — but that did not make it any easier for Gail Jones to accept.

She began to feel increasingly bitter towards her husband. Why couldn't they settle in one place? What was it about him that made him such a wanderer? But then the grass is always greener on the other side when you are feeling depressed. Gail was subconsciously blaming her husband for all her emotional problems. It was a tinderbox scenario, liable to explode into a crescendo of bitterness at any moment, and Graham Jones was painfully aware of his wife's unhappiness.

That was why, in September, 1981, he decided that moving around Britain as a time-and-motion man was no longer the perfect career for him. He unselfishly decided that his wife and children came before his job — and he started to look around for a new profession. Graham Jones had always had a dream about running a seaside pub. It was something he had frequently discussed with Gail, but they had always dismissed it as just the wishful thinking of someone stuck in a totally different kind of job. But now he had an opportunity to make that fantasy come true. Graham Jones decided now was the time to try and have the place of his dreams.

By this time, the Jones family had settled in the gritty Yorkshire town of Wetherby. A grey-stoned place filled with friendly, hard-working people whose idea of a good time was a regular pint at their local hostelry. For months Graham Jones searched desperately for the perfect tavern to run but — besides a lack of seaside — there just wasn't anywhere suitable.

Then he decided to look slightly further afield. The craggy Yorkshire coastline had dozens of little towns and villages. There had to be somewhere. Jones knew that the sooner he found a pub to run, the sooner Gail might start to emerge from her self-imposed depression. The clock that represented the survival of their marriage was ticking away at a fast rate. He was well aware that it would not survive for much longer.

Graham Jones knew the moment he saw the outside of the *Belle Vue Hotel* that it was the perfect place for him and his young family. Situated right near the seaside in the small community of Filey, Yorkshire, it

71

just had that instant kind of effect on him. This was truly what he had dreamed of doing for his entire adult life. Now those ambitions were about to become a reality. He felt so relieved that they could at last settle in one place.

Filey itself was a dour-looking place filled with lots of red and grey brick buildings. Row upon row of tiny terraced cottages off the seafront. A scattering of shops and pubs, and a sleepy atmosphere encouraged most mornings by the thick mist that swept in from the cruel North Sea. A blanket of cloud often filled the sky, turning the sea into a musty green colour that deceived the mind into believing it would not be very pleasant to swim in. The truth was that many locals took to the sea on summer mornings and it had a fantastically refreshing effect on anyone who bothered to brave the cold water.

Within days of viewing the *Belle Vue*, Graham Jones and his young family were happily installed in the double-fronted property that was a truly imposing sight on the seafront. As Graham and Gail looked out at the North Sea from their bay-fronted living room above the hotel bar, they felt a resurgence of the warmth and loving they had experienced all those years earlier on that cruise where they had first met.

Now at last they were back by the sea — the very place that had sparked their romance in the first place. Graham and Gail used to joke about going on another cruise to help revive their often flagging relationship. But now they had a permanent place by the sea and Graham Jones presumed that he had now sealed their marriage for life.

For the next two years Graham and Gail really did take their task at the *Belle Vue* to heart. It was just the sort of joint challenge that they had obviously needed since the cracks in their marriage first began to appear. The problems of their previous few years were soon put behind them as they started to build the hostelry into a very popular haunt for locals.

Graham got himself a reputation as a warm, caring landlord for whom nothing was too much trouble. When he started running the local football team it was yet another dream come true for him. He had always been a keen sportsman and now he had become a truly accepted member of this tightly knit Yorkshire community.

And there was an added bonus from all this — all the members of the team and their hundreds of fans naturally came to make the *Belle Vue* their regular venue for a pint and a chat about their favorite football teams.

Gail was also feeling far more settled. She was enjoying the challenge of setting up the pub just as much as her husband. It was very hard work with exceptionally long hours, but the bonuses were there for everyone to see — a huge place overlooking the sea, a husband who was always around. Happy, peaceful, safe surroundings where kids could play in the streets and parks without fear of attack.

Gail also rediscovered a pride in herself. She enjoyed it when some of the younger male customers tried to flirt with her. It helped her regain her confidence. She felt a bit like she did all those years earlier when the crew members on that cruise had flattered her.

"Don't forget, Gail. I'll be waiting when you decide to leave Graham."

Comments like this were just harmless quips that summed up the happy-go-lucky atmosphere the Jones had managed to foster on their premises. Gail did not take any of them seriously and Graham just laughed whenever he heard them. It was just part and parcel of life running a tavern.

Mind you, some of them did try to take things a little further sometimes. They were the customers who'd try and pinch Gail's still very-firm-bottom when she was leaning over them to pick up some glasses. Most of the time she would give them a rather evil look and they'd get the message. But some of them did not.

These were the ones who were really getting off on the sight of the pretty brunette mother-of-two who tended to dress in a tight-fitting pencil skirt with a low-cut blouse and high heels. But just so long as they did not actually try anything sexual with her, there was nothing that she could do apart from glare back at them.

One particular "pest", however, had a different sort of effect on Gail. His name was Rod Tillotson and he became a regular in the *Belle Vue* about a year after the Joneses arrived.

Gail could often feel his eyes giving her body the once-over as she walked away from his table, having collected some glasses. Sometimes their eyes would meet and she would immediately turn away, embarrassed at having caught his glance. Somehow, she reacted differently to this man. She could handle most of them, but there was something about Rod Tillotson that made her a little uneasy.

At first she thought nothing of it. But when he started to come into the pub virtually every night and pour out his troubles to her, she started to realise what it was. Unlike all the other pushy guys, Rod was one hell of a ruggedly handsome fellow. His mop of thick black hair and his droopy moustache made him look more like some Mexican bandit than an unemployed labourer. And he seemed to have experienced such tragedy in his life. She soon found herself listening intently to his account of his broken marriage and his current life — living in a tiny council flat in Filey with his elderly parents. She could not help feeling a bit sorry for him. She also managed to ignore the sneering remarks of the other locals:

"Gail. You'd better watch out for Rod, he's a real ladies man."

"I think he's sniffing after you, Gail. He's one hell of a womaniser."

74

Basically, those regular customers were saying exactly what Graham Jones was thinking. He had recognised Tillotson as an unscrupulous type of character but he did not want to cause a row with his wife, so he let those regulars do his talking for him.

Just so long as Tillotson did not try anything on with his wife, then he was reasonably content to let her continue those long heart-to-heart chats with Rod most evenings.

"I don't think that's a very good idea, do you?"

Graham Jones's reaction when his wife asked him if they could hire Rod Tillotson as a barman was hardly surprising. But Gail felt so sorry for the six-foot labourer. He had spent months telling her about his desperate attempts to find a job. It was only natural that he should end up asking her if there was any chance of a barman's position at the *Belle Vue*.

"I feel we owe it to him. He's a good bloke."

Gail Jones's opinion of Tillotson was the complete opposite to that of every other customer of the hostelry, but she seemed genuinely concerned about his well-being. In any case, Graham Jones did not want a row about it. He had heard the gossip and seen the danger signs but then again, they did need more staff. The pub was packed out every night, and he and his wife were finding it exhausting just keeping the basics of the business together.

When Rod Tillotson turned up for his first day of work behind the bar at the *Belle Vue*, there were sniggers all around from the customers. But Gail Jones was happy. In fact she was happier than she had ever felt throughout her marriage. As she walked down from their flat above the bar, her eyes locked straight onto Tillotson and she smiled. Now she had almost everything she ever wanted...

At first, Tillotson only worked a few days a week at

the tavern. That meant there were only rare chances for more of those heart-to-heart chats between him and Gail. But they still managed to brush by each other dozens of times each day behind that crowded bar.

Gail would stop momentarily whenever their paths crossed. Only long enough for a heart beat, but it was sufficient to encourage Tillotson in his quest for the inevitable. She did not really know why she was doing it. She just enjoyed being close to him. Sometimes their hands would touch as he leant behind her to get a glass out of the dishwasher. On other occasions, their finger-tips would connect as they both tried to get change out of the till.

Graham Jones did not really notice those first danger signs. Maybe he just did not want to know. But the locals in the *Belle Vue* wanted to know everything. They loved to wind up "the two lovebirds" as they liked to call them. Gail would blush heavily whenever a customer made any reference to hunky Tillotson. The part-time barman adored the attention. He wanted her to know his eventual intentions, and this was the best way of getting the message across loud and clear.

Even the Joneses' two children, Helen, 5, and Karen, 8, were falling for the charms of Tillotson. He had a daughter, who lived with his ex-wife in Manchester so he knew how to handle kids. It wasn't long before Graham Jones reluctantly asked his wife's admirer if he could work full time for them.

Then the would-be romeo managed to convince Gail to allow him to partner her in the local pool team. At first, she resisted his suggestion because she knew it would upset Graham, but when Tillotson pleaded she gave in. There was something about him that she was finding increasingly difficult to resist. She knew she was being sucked in, but she thought she could contain her emotions sufficiently to maintain a distance.

Tillotson was getting more and more obsessed with

76

Gail. After they formed a winning pool partnership, he often used to find himself lusting after her as she leaned over a pool table to pot a difficult shot. He would imagine what he would like to do to her if the opportunity ever arose. It was hardly surprising when it did...

Gail Jones was just locking up the double-doors to the *Belle Vue*'s lounge bar after the last customer had left the premises, when she turned to see Rod Tillotson staring at her across the cluttered room. Her husband was away visiting his sick and elderly mother in the south of England. She knew that she was vulnerable. She sort of expected it to happen. Now she was facing the very man who wanted to steal her away from her husband — and there was absolutely no-one around to prevent the inevitable from occurring.

For a few moments they stood there in silence. Gail felt a tremble run up her spine. No words were exchanged between them. Just feelings. Thoughts. Intentions. She walked towards him.

Within seconds they were locked in a passionate embrace. She felt him wrap his arms around her. They pressed so hard together. Afraid that if either of them let go, then something might happen to stop them carrying on.

She ran her hand through his thick mane of hair over and over. Pulling his face closer and closer. Their tongues exploring each other's mouths. Their hands stroking, exploring one another properly for the first time.

Then she nuzzled her mouth into his neck and nipped his skin with her teeth. Each time it brought a gasp of pleasure from Rod. Then his hands moved down the front of her blouse and squeezed tightly on her firm breasts. He could just feel one of her nipples protruding through the lacy bra. It was peeping through the blackness like a little pink strawberry, ripe and ready to be eaten.

He dipped his head down and sucked at that nipple through the bra. She could feel a wonderful sensation as he sucked just a little harder each time. Her own mouth had by now connected with his ears. Pushing her tongue in and out. Then she sucked the air out ever so carefully for maximum pleasure and minimum pain.

They were on the bare vinyl floor now. Completely lost in their own passionate world. The grim surroundings did not matter. The cold bare surface could have been anywhere in the universe.

He pushed her tight-fitting skirt up to expose her bare thighs to the crisp night air and carefully prised her legs apart before letting his hands explore her inner sanctum. She was moaning softly now. Her eyes were closed momentarily as she envisaged the love-making that was about to happen.

She grabbed him through his trousers with her hand and squeezed and stroked him. They were locked in a sexual frenzy from which there was no retreat. She lifted her bottom off that sticky floor surface to allow him to remove her panties. Then she heard the sound of his zip fastener undoing...

After it was over, they lay silent in each other's arms. The eerie silence of the night enveloped them after more than an hour of heated passion. Every now and again, the headlights of a passing car would drift across the ceiling of the bar before disappearing into the shadows.

He looked into her eyes and kissed her full on the lips. It was the ultimate evidence of his love for her. A long, lingering kiss after sex is something that only true lovers ever experience.

Gail looked up at the bar behind her and thought of all the hard work, time and energy that had gone into making the *Belle Vue* so successful and promised herself: I am not going to lose this. Whatever happens, I am not going to give it up.

Over the next few months the inevitable occurred. Gail and Tillotson grew closer and closer. Snatching secret moments together when Graham Jones was out of the bar. Their love-making grew more and more intense. He had opened up a whole new world of sexual experimentation for Gail. It was something she had never experienced during more than ten years of marriage.

It couldn't go on for ever though. People were starting to talk.

Just like a classic office romance, all the tell-tale signs were showing. The warm smiles across a crowded bar. The little kisses on the neck as they squeezed past each other. The never-ending closeness wherever they happened to be.

"You dirty bugger. We know what you're up to."

The regulars were all pretty blunt characters. It did not take them long to work out what was happening between Gail and Tillotson. It wasn't really moral indignation that sparked their comments. More a combination of jealousy — because many of them thought Gail was a very attractive woman — and a sense of protectiveness towards Graham Jones, whom they all considered to be a "good bloke".

As is so often the case, it was the husband who was the last one to realise that his wife's friendship with the barman had blossomed into an out-and-out affair. But when he confronted her with his suspicions, she looked him straight in the face and said:

"Don't be daft, Graham. I wouldn't do that to you."

"But everyone's saying it and I've seen the way you look at him."

"How can you even take any notice of bar gossip? Who d'you believe most — a bunch of customers or your own wife?"

Graham Jones hesitated for a moment. The choice was simple: gossip or denial.

"Well, you of course."

No sooner had he said it than he knew he would

79

grow to regret it. If only he had known that he had just sealed his own fate...

"You must be bloody joking."

Rod Tillotson thought he was hearing things when Gail Jones first suggested they should murder her husband. They were sitting in a little coffee shop a few miles from the *Belle Vue*, snatching some time together, when she said it.

"We've got to do it."

He could see from the coldness in her eyes that she meant business, but he had no intention of committing the ultimate crime.

"Forget it. Why don't we just run off together?"

Gail Jones dropped the subject for the moment. But she knew the time would come when her secret lover could be persuaded. In actual fact, it took a few more sex sessions and a whole lot more emotional blackmail to do it.

Then the handsome barman did more than just agree to help her commit murder, he came up with a fail-safe idea that he was convinced would help them get away with "the perfect crime".

Graham Jones was poring over his vast stamp collection when he heard a shout from the bar downstairs, where he'd left Gail and Tillotson to run the tavern while he retired early.

"Gail's fainted. Can you help, Graham?"

The barman's plea for assistance seemed perfectly reasonable, and Graham bounded down the stairs to help revive his pretty wife who lay slumped at the foot of the steps.

As he leant down to check her pulse, he did not even see the pick-axe handle swinging ominously in his direction. The first blow crushed his skull as if it were putty. As Graham Jones turned, he just caught a glance of Tillotson before he smashed the wooden weapon into his head a second time.

Blow after blow came crashing down on Jones's skull. At one stage, the pick-axe handle got wedged in between the cavities of his brain and Tillotson had to pull it as if it were jammed in a piece of rock. After each crushing blow, he stopped for a few seconds to recover his composure before continuing. It must have been mentally, as well as physically agonising for Jones because each time he struggled up, in the vain hope that the attack was over. But it was not going to end until he was well and truly dead.

Upstairs the Joneses' two innocent daughters slept on — completely unaware that their mother and her secret lover were cold-bloodedly taking the life of their beloved father.

Downstairs, the twelfth and last blow was being inflicted as Graham Jones lay in a puddle of his own blood, his head cracked open in little pieces like an eggshell. In silence, Tillotson disappeared upstairs to change his clothes so that there was no evidence to link him to the killing. Meanwhile, Gail emptied the bar till as part of their carefully planned charade to convince the police they had been the innocent victims of a robbery that had gone tragically wrong.

Tillotson then returned downstairs with orders for Gail that truly tested her love for the well-built barman.

"Make sure you hit me really hard. This has got to look good."

Gail shut her eyes tightly and started to smash that same pick-axe handle down on her lusty lover's head. She could not do it. She had just witnessed the brutal killing of her own husband, but this was far more distressing for her. She desperately did not want to hurt the man she loved.

"Just do it, Gail."

She had no choice and she knew it. She used all her strength to swipe the wooden weapon down hard on his head. It knocked him off balance and he fell down a short flight of stairs to the hallway below.

"Now the glasses."

Gail got a tray of glasses from the bar and dropped the whole lot over her lover as he lay there amongst the smears·of blood on the vinyl. Mission accomplished.

The perfect robbery scene had now been set: the battered, dead, heroic husband; and the barman who tried to fight off his assailants, but ended up getting a beating himself.

Gail rubbed her hands together with satisfaction as she looked down at her moaning, groaning lover and the fragments of her husband's skull lying on the floor nearby.

The death of Graham Jones made headline news throughout the country. His brutal, senseless killing was followed by a vast police manhunt for his murderers. But detectives were far from happy. There was something about the crime that did not seem right, but they couldn't put their fingers on it.

When officers insisted on searching the entire *Belle Vue* tavern, Gail looked on curiously but showed no emotion or fear. Tillotson had said the police would never be able to prove it, just so long as they stuck to their story and there was no evidence lying around.

She watched as they took fragments of the glasses she had dropped over her lover's head away for finger printing, slightly puzzled as to why they were even bothering to take prints off glasses used by the customers.

As the officers headed up the stairs towards the bedrooms, she suddenly remembered something — the pick-axe handle was still under the mattress of the bed she had once shared with her loving husband Graham. She did not know what to do. She knew they would be sure to find it. She paced up and down by the main bar. Waiting for the call.

The inevitable happened within minutes when she saw a detective gingerly carrying the weapon down the stairs. Her heart nearly jumped through her mouth, but she kept remembering what Tillotson had said:

"Play it cool. Don't admit anything."

The officer who approached her looked bemused.

"Why do you keep this under your bed, Mrs Jones?"

She had to think fast.

"Protection. We've always been careful in case of robbers."

The detective then did something that Gail could not believe. He did not follow through with any more questions. There was an uncomfortable silence as she waited to be accused of her husband's murder, but it never came. Instead, he said:

"At least you'll be relieved to hear that this isn't the murder weapon. We believe your husband was killed with a metal bar."

Gail could not believe what she was hearing. But she certainly was not about to complain!

Within a few more minutes the police search of the pub was complete and the officers retreated from the premises, leaving Gail Jones to clean up the bar and prepare for opening time. It was business as usual at the *Belle Vue* that day.

That afternoon, Gail Jones took that wooden pick-axe handle and began a bizarre bid to excommunicate it from her life. She knew that it was only a matter of time before the police realised that it had in fact been the murder weapon — and then they'd be back searching for it.

So, first she chopped it up into tiny pieces. The plan had been to just chuck it in the rubbish, but that police search party earlier had scared her considerably. They might come back and find it. No, she thought to herself, it's got to literally disappear.

For some weird reason (no-one knows exactly why), Gail Jones then tried to cook the remains of that pick-axe handle in her electric cooker at the *Belle Vue*. When she realised that it might start a fire, she abandoned that scheme and sat down, exhausted, to try and work out another way to get rid of the pick-axe handle, which now lay in charred bits in an oven pan in front of her.

Then she worked it out. It was so obvious. It had been staring her in the face all along. The sea was the place to dispose of the weapon.

A few hours later, in an extraordinary scene that strangely resembled the scattering of a loved one's ashes, Gail Jones stood on the cliffs at nearby Flamborough Head and watched as the burnt bits of wood descended slowly down to the sea below. They would never sink, but at least they would be dispersed forever.

Back in Filey, the rumourmongers were working over-time. It seemed as if everyone except the police had already judged Gail and Tillotson guilty of murdering her husband.

"It's so bloody obvious. They staged the whole thing."

It might have been obvious but there wasn't a shred of real evidence... yet.

The policeman leading the murder hunt, Det. Supt. Strickland Carter, was feeling a mite frustrated to say the least. He knew all about the gossip in Filey and he was just as convinced as all the locals, but he had to be patient. The results of all those forensic tests had not come back yet. They would just have to wait.

It was another few days until the police got what they wanted. Traces of blood found on Tillotson's shoes matched Graham Jones's blood, as did similar blood spots found on Gail's clothes.

But most crucial of all, police were able to prove that the glasses thrown over Tillotson came from an upstairs bar *not* the main lounge bar on the ground floor.

Confronted with the evidence, the two illicit lovers were arrested but still insisted they were innocent.

At their trial at York Crown Court in June, 1985, Gail Jones and Rod Tillotson were found guilty of murder and sentenced to life in prison.

The pretty brunette collapsed in tears as sentence was pronounced, and two women prison officers had to carry her back to her cell while a doctor and an ambulance were called.

After the case, Chief Supt Carter said: "She was play-acting from beginning to end. She was arrested because she overreacted and I had a gut feeling she was putting on a show. She maintained it to the end, right down to the stage-managed collapse in the dock."

6

The Woman In Black

The tiny villages scattered around the Yorkshire town of Rotherham consist of tightly knit communities where absolutely nothing goes unnoticed. The local pub and the corner shop are still the places where residents exchange pleasantries and gossip, just as they have been doing for more than a hundred years.

Coal mining is still the most important source of income in the area. Its influence can be felt throughout the area — from the blackened faces that emerge from the mines after a gruelling day's work to the neat terraces of homes built in Victorian times for the forefathers of those very same miners.

The village of Wath was a classic example. Cobbled streets still remained as a warm reminder of the days when the only means of transport was a pony and trap. Early mornings were, as more often than not, dominated by the damp mist that seemed to descend on the village like a vast blanket, waiting for the heat of the sun to burn it away. At about that time each weekday, the men in those tiny households would emerge for yet another gruelling day down the pits. If they were lucky, they'd get to walk down the street in the company of one of their children, employed to deliver the tabloid newspapers that were often a family's' only real link with the outside world.

But by 1984, modern times had begun to catch up with life in places like Wath. Most families still relied on mining as their main source of income, but there was a disturbing element creeping into the once-solid-as-a-rock community — crime. For more years than anyone cared to remember, Wath had been pretty much a crime-free zone. Certainly a few apples were stolen and maybe the odd pint of milk from a doorstep, but nothing more serious than that.

However, the greed and cunning that seemed to

come as part of the Margaret Thatcher economic package in the early 1980s, was inevitably heading for places like Wath. It might have arrived a few years after most of the rest of the country, but it got there all the same.

That was how PC Pat Durkin found himself transferred to the once-non-existent Wath Police Station. Now, it was hardly a hotbed of activity; but the very fact that the Yorkshire Constabulary considered it necessary to increase the quota of uniformed officers covering the area was proof in itself. The threat of serious crime had reared its ugly head.

PC Pat was the sort of police officer every community prays for. With his dark hair and medium-length sideburns, he had a friendly, warm manner that truly endeared him to the community. What made him even more acceptable to them was the fact that he had been a coal miner himself until his mid-twenties.

And to cap matters, when he arrived in Wath, PC Durkin came amid stories of incredible bravery that threatened to turn him into a comic-book-style hero overnight.

Back in 1978, he had received an award after rescuing a woman in a coma from a blazing inferno. PC Durkin had kicked open the door of Mrs Barbara Matthewman's smoke-filled flat in Rawmarsh and battled through the dense, choking smoke to try and find her. For many minutes he wandered blindly through the stench and fumes to seek out Mrs Matthewman. Then he grabbed the 25-year-old woman and pulled her to safety.

Afterwards it emerged that she had been in a diabetic coma and if it had not been for PC Durkin's outstanding courage she would almost certainly have died. Incredibly, the gutsy officer then went back in to the flat once more to help put out the blaze before it spread to any of the nearby homes.

You could certainly say that by the time PC Durkin

arrived in Wath his reputation was second to none. Locals welcomed him as one of their own. And he had no intention of shattering their illusions just as long as he walked the beat of their cobbled streets.

She was tall, blonde and very shapely. Her hair flowed like the waves on a choppy ocean. The curls seemed to bounce, as she walked uprightly and confidently. Her eyes were deep and sensuous, always probing beneath the surface like a reptile sizing up its prey. Her hips were wide, but not so big as to put off any likely suitor. They just gave the impression that she was strong in every sense of the word. Capable of taking on whatever any man had to offer.

But then Diana Jade Perry was a very headstrong 25-year-old woman. She enjoyed her work as a clerk in the Department of Health and Social Security office in Wath. Diana felt a certain sense of power because her job at the DHSS gave her a unique insight into the community she lived in. She knew who was out of work or why someone was fired. But best of all she knew which men in the community were just lazy no hopers trying desperately to avoid a real job at all costs.

Diana also got a thrill out of seeing some of those unemployed men studying her as they queued up for dole money. But then it was hardly surprising that she caused a little stir. Compared to her dowdy workmates, Diana looked like a beauty queen. She tended to dress all in black. One of her favourite outfits was a figure-hugging dress that clung to her like a glove. Rounded off with distinctive five-inch stiletto heels, she really did cut quite a sight in that drab, grey office.

Sometimes she would give some of those men a little flash of thigh as her tight-fitting skirt rode up her legs while she moved position at her desk. She could feel all their eyes feasting upon her and it gave her a very nice sensation. Nothing too sordid, just a tingle in the right places.

But one of the problems with Wath was that it tended to be a very quiet place for an active, lively person like Diana Perry. She increasingly found herself getting more excitement out of those harmless interludes in the office than anything she could do in her own spare time.

She hated the local pubs because they were still very male-orientated places where single, sexy women like Diana were looked upon as intruders into a masculine world of darts and chit-chat about soccer and rugby league. Often she would sit at home in her tiny flat in Church Street, opposite the police station in Wath, and watch those handsome bobbies in their dark blue uniforms going in and out. Then she would settle in front of the television and tune in to her favourite shows like *Coronation Street* and *Crossroads* and try to imagine what life might be like in a more glamorous location.

But as the months progressed, she became increasingly bored with the lack of social opportunities in Wath. At 25, she was almost over the hill in marriage terms. Most women took their wedding vows no later than their early twenties in a place like Wath. Diana was seriously worried that she would never find Mr Right. And then there were the more basic emotions, like feeling the need to have a man sexually. Certainly she had enjoyed a good time with men over the years, but there seemed to be a real lack of available males in Wath. She wanted someone with a little edge. A little daring. She used to fantasise at night sometimes about that perfect knight in shining armour who would sweep her off her feet and ravish her and satisfy her every demand.

Diana was starting to spend more and more time watching those good-looking bobbies over the road. Some evenings she would spend ages discreetly peeping through the curtains, trying to work out which one she liked best. Then she would at least go to bed with the features of that handsome face and uniform stamped in her memory. It wasn't the same as the real thing but it would have to do — for the moment.

"I'm sorry to trouble you, but I've gone and locked myself out of my flat over the road. Could you help?"

It was a dream come true for Diana Perry when she found the perfect excuse to turn her fantasies into reality. As she stood pouting slightly in front of PC Pat Durkin, she knew instantly that he was the one for her.

"No problem. I'll come over and see what I can do."

Pat Durkin could not help giving her an admiring glance as he cast his eyes up and down her body. That tight-fitting black dress really showed off her curves. But there was something familiar about her. He hesitated for a moment and then remembered. A few days earlier, he and a colleague had seen her going into the block of flats opposite.

"That looks like a bit of fun, Pat."

His colleague had always had an eye for the girls. Now PC Durkin couldn't wait to tell him the next day whose flat he'd been into.

As Diana and her knight in shining armour headed for the exit to the police station, the station sergeant called after him:

"Pat. You take as long as you like, mate."

Diana Perry knew exactly what the implication was, but she did not care. She already felt that unique tingle of sexual excitement flowing through her body.

PC Pat Durkin also knew that this was going to end up being more than just a plain old boring domestic call. He sensed the moment she walked into the station that something would happen between them. And, as he watched her body clinging ever so tightly to that black dress as they walked up the stairs to the flat, he knew that they would connect.

After all, he was not married any more. His wife Jenny had long since departed. In fact, it had been a very distressing time for all concerned because she had suffered a fairly nasty nervous breakdown. Luckily for PC Durkin, no-one took any notice of Jenny's accusations that he had driven her to insanity because of his insatiable appetite for sex of any description. The doctors said she was suffering from delusions. How could a respectable police officer be committing the sort of sickening sex acts she was accusing him of?

Even when Mrs Durkin tried to make the doctors go to their house to see the weapons of sexual destruction he used on her, they ignored her. The hysterical outbursts. The crazy accusations. They were all indicative of a seriously deluded woman. PC Durkin just stood firm and smiled politely whenever the doctors tried to bring up the subject of his own sexual preferences. Luckily, they were too embarrassed to push the situation.

When Mrs Durkin was committed indefinitely to a mental hospital it seemed the kindest thing to do in the circumstances. PC Durkin quietly and tactfully filed for divorce, and the subject of his first marriage became hidden behind a veil of secrecy that no-one dared try to penetrate.

"Poor Pat. He must have had a rough time."

That was about the nearest anyone ever came to referring to Jenny Durkin. And that was the way PC Durkin planned to keep it.

Back at the front door to Diana Perry's flat that evening in the winter of 1984, PC Durkin was starting to get those urges again for the first time in years. As he fiddled with the front door lock in a bid to open it for her, he felt his hand shaking with expectation. This might well be the perfect one for him.

Diana saw his hesitancy and took it to mean that Durkin was just as aware of the chemistry between them as she was. Their hands touched as he twisted

91

and turned the lock until the door finally fell open. She had engineered the meeting she so desperately wanted. Now the next stage was to lure him into her life. It would not take long.

The first few occasions they had sex it was warm, romantic and very satisfying. He seemed to be able to switch her on from any one of a hundred different parts of her body. She had lusted after him in an animal fashion. It was the first time in her entire life that the object of her fantasies had become a reality.

She liked to make him keep his well pressed, dark blue uniform on until the last possible moment. Then she would pull the silver buttons so hard they would pop undone as she searched for his chest and nipples to feast upon.

PC Durkin played along with her happily. He always enjoyed straight sex the first few times with a woman. But he knew there would come a time when he would want to try something different. Always in the back of his mind he was scheming some sick and twisted act.

Meanwhile two rather lonely people stuck in a grey, quiet mining community in the middle of Yorkshire were devouring each other with the sort of sexual expertise few would ever experience in a lifetime. They were definitely two lost souls looking for something to break the monotony of life. PC Durkin laughed quietly to himself as he thought of his colleagues working hard at the station across the road, and then turned towards Diana and began kissing her neck uncontrollably.

She returned the passion by pulling his hair so that his head went lower. Then she stuck out her breasts so that he could not avoid licking and sucking them. He enjoyed her forcefulness. He thought it might be a clue to the sort of sex they would eventually enjoy together. But for the moment this would do.

As she pushed him further down below her breasts and past her tummy button, she could feel the burning passion reaching a crescendo. She wanted him to use his tongue as the ultimate weapon of pleasure. This surely must be love and lust wrapped into one, she thought. No-one could create such extraordinary sensations and not feel strongly for his partner.

The climax became all the more intense as she lay there thinking about her future with a man whose first wife lay strapped to a bed in a nearby mental hospital.

"Let's move in together."

Diana Perry had taken the words right out of her lover's mouth. He had been longing to build up the courage to ask her but now she had beaten him to the line.

"Get your things together and we'll move you in tonight."

Diana could not quite believe her ears. This really was becoming a dream come true. All the lust and passion of the previous few weeks had brought them both to the same conclusion — for completely different reasons.

PC Durkin — the hero cop with a soft touch — was certain she would do whatever he asked. This time, there would be no nervous breakdowns. No hysterical outbursts at the most crucial moments. Diana had been primed to be his love slave. She was so besotted by him that he was convinced she would do anything. In any case, she was hardly an innocent bystander herself.

She had confessed to the policeman that she had certain sexual desires that he might find offensive. He tried to assure her that as far as he was concerned, "anything goes". But Diana Perry's idea of sexual adventure was not in the same league as the man she had just agreed to share a home with.

As she moved all her things into his comfortable, spacious flat nearby in Sivilla Road, Kilnhurst, word soon spread about the "woman in black". Neighbours could not help noticing her in her expensive designer outfits that were always only one colour.

Kilnhurst was a similar sort of community to Wath. The same priorities. The same prejudices. The same bleakness. But PC Durkin was much happier now that he had got her out of that flat opposite the police station in Wath. He wanted to ensure that she was not tempted to wonder in the direction of any other bobbies. Her confession that she adored the police uniform he wore made Durkin wonder just how easily she might stray if tempted. Also, he knew he could never carry out the full extent of his sexual obsessions in a flat just a few yards from where his colleagues worked.

But Diana Perry had one hobby that she did not really mention to her policeman lover during the first few lustful weeks of their relationship. Her love of wearing black had a deeper significance because she was fascinated by Nazi regalia and by the workings of the extreme right-wing political organisation, the National Front.

At a time when Britain was in the middle of an immigration crisis that threatened to tear the country apart, Diana considered herself very much a blue-blooded Aryan who disapproved of the hard-working Asians and West Indians who had settled in Yorkshire over the previous twenty years.

To start with, she did not mention her feelings to PC Durkin in case it put a damper on their love affair. But she still continued buying Nazi mementos at a shop in Rotherham. When the time was right, she would show him all her trophies. But, for the moment, she was worried that he might get the wrong impression from the jackboots, the helmets and the leather jackets — not to mention the literature that spoke in vivid detail about cleansing the world of all its so-called impurity.

But her obsession with all these trophies from the sickest regime in the history of the world had been

IN COLD BLOOD:
Author Wensley Clarkson with Kathy Gaultney inside the
Dwight Correctional Institute in Illinios.

IN COLD BLOOD:
Drug baron Roy Vernon Dean, who lured Kathy Gaultney into the narotics business.

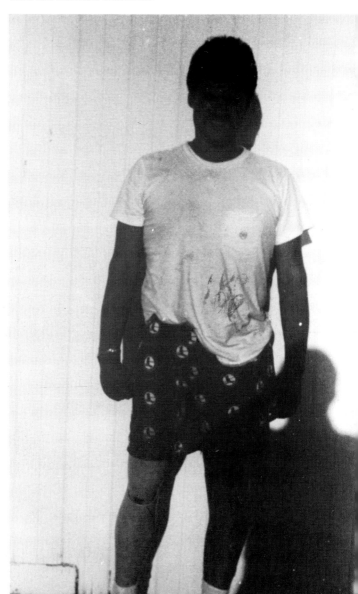

IN COLD BLOOD:

Top: Mary O'Guinn, who became Kathy Gaultney's boss in their drug ring.

Below: The so-called 'Death Cottage' at the Dwight Correctional Institute where Kathy Gaultney and at least twenty other women killers are imprisoned.

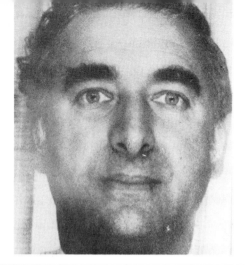

UNDER THE WILLOW TREE

Top: Brutal husband Tom Scotland, whose vicious treatment of his wife June, (*below right*), and daughter Caroline, (*below left*), led them to kill.

Ricky Rogers

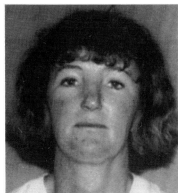

Diana Bogdanoff

Brian Stafford

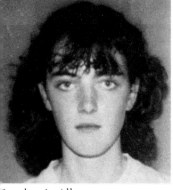

Stephanie Allen

NAKED FEAR:
The four killers in the outrageous nudist beach contract
killing of Phil Bogdanoff -
(*bottom right*).

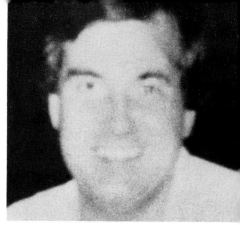

THE SEASIDE KILLERS:

Top: Seaside killers' victim Graham Jones.

Bottom: Handsome lover Rod Tillotson, whose lust for Gail Jones turned him into a cold blooded killer.

THE SEASIDE KILLERS:

Top: Gail Jones whose bitterness towards her husband drove her to murder.

Below: The Belle View Hotel, where Jones and Tillotson committed their horrendous crime.

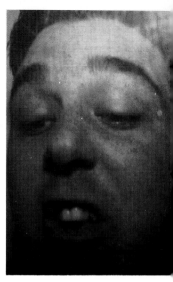

THE ROOT OF ALL EVIL :

Top left: Julie Cheema - the two-timing wife, who sentenced her sick husband, Mohinder, to death.

Top right: Neil Markley - the 19 year old, whose affair with Julie Cheema helped hatch their murderous plot.

Bottom: The off-licence in Hounslow, Middx, where Mohinder Cheema was gunned down twice.

growing all the time. A year earlier she decided she wanted to start collecting German weapons of destruction. Her first purchase was a 9mm Luger pistol.

On the day she bought it she took it home, unwrapped the packaging and just looked at it for several minutes. Admiring its shape and size. She stroked it gently and felt the coldness of the metal on her fingertips. Some days, she would take it to her lips and kiss the barrel softly and sensuously.

She could not wait for her lover to get home later that evening. She had decided that the time had come to tell him about her fantasies. She pushed the end of that Luger barrel a few inches into her mouth and sucked it hard and let her mind wander forward to the love and passion they would most definitely experience that night.

When PC Pat Durkin got back to his steaming love-nest that evening, he got just the sort of surprise he had been longing for. He had refrained from confessing his own sexual obsessions to her, in the hope that he could gradually introduce them to her as their appetite for outrageous lust increased.

Now, his beautiful blonde girlfriend was telling him about her own sexual habits and it was like holding a red rag to a bull. Durkin felt a surge of sexual excitement stream through his body as she told him about her fascination with the Nazis and her substantial collection of memorabilia. He thought he knew then that no amount of sexual force would be too much for her.

As her hand crept up his blue-trousered leg and began probing and squeezing, he felt the rush of adrenalin. This time they would do everything humanly possible in the name of love.

Diana Perry pulled the black leather jackboots up and just over her knees. They were easy to get on over the sheer black stockings, and the three dark shades seemed to complement her body so perfectly. As his eyes panned up from the black leather to the grey silk to the black cotton of her garter belt, he took a deep breath and absorbed the living fantasy before his very eyes.

"Now bend over."

PC Durkin did not sound very forceful in his command the first time around. He knew he needed to be stronger. He looked her straight in the eyes and repeated the instruction:

"Bend over *now*!"

Diana Perry had not meant it to end up like this. She had seen her sexual Nazi-style outfit as part of foreplay before a straight sexual encounter. But now her lover was expecting something more. She hesitated for a moment before acknowledging that he obviously meant business. Her love for him was so strong that she decided to let him do whatever he wanted.

She bent over the end of the bed and waited for that first crack of the whip which he held so firmly in his hand.

The first few lashes were not too hard, so she just bit her lip and decided that it would soon be over and then they could both devour each other like they had done so often in the past. But PC Durkin had other ideas on his mind. This was only the beginning.

The next half-dozen lashes were much harder and they left deep weals in her flesh. She tried to get up after each one, but he pushed her down forcefully and told her:

"Don't move or I'll have to punish you even more."

Diana was scared now. Each slash was more painful than the last and she could hear the trembling of excitement in his voice. She knew that he would not stop until he was satisfied.

Yet, incredibly, her love for him dominated her mind even at that awful moment. She felt as if she had somehow caused the pain by encouraging him to think those evil thoughts. She got sexual excitement out of wearing those outfits, so the natural next stage was to get involved in sadism of some kind. But she did not like being hurt and she was unsure what to think of a man who so dearly wanted to cause so much pain and suffering.

By the time he eventually stopped, the agony was so great that she was crying real tears of fear. But he did not care. He simply turned her over and forced himself on her. Even then, she kept thinking: "It's all my fault. It's all my fault."

As the months went by, Diana Perry got more and more confused by her relationship with PC Pat Durkin. One side of her wanted to feel disgust for him, while the other side admired his daytime persona — that of a loving, trusting servant of law and order. Despite repeated abuse at his hands, she felt somehow that she was getting what she deserved.

She dearly wished she had never dressed up in those Nazi jackboots that first night, but she could not turn the clock back and he was all she had. Now, he forced her to wear the same slinky costumes that she had once so enjoyed putting on to tease and tantalise him.

But his beatings were getting worse and worse. The whips were used virtually every night, and then he would make her do things that she never even dreamt of in her wildest fantasies. Some nights he would come home armed to the teeth with an assortment of sex aids, like vibrators and dildos. And those were the nights when the sex was still relatively gentle. Diana was not a prudish person and she liked experimenting, just so long as it was mutually enjoyable. After all, there was little else to do in Kilnhurst.

The sex aids seemed to divert him from inflicting pain and suffering. And Diana's unswerving love was starting to take on a much more serious dimension. As the beatings subsided, she began to wonder if perhaps there was a chance they could live happily ever after.

She still had no idea that PC Durkin's first wife

was locked up inside a mental hospital after the torture she had suffered at the hands of her brutal husband.

"Come on. Let's do it now."

For once, this was not PC Pat Durkin demanding that his live-in lover agree to yet more sex. This time, the couple were on a rare outing together in the nearby town of Rotherham. It was mid-November, and the biting gusts of wind blowing off the nearby moors were making her curly hair sweep from her face to reveal its slightly rounded contours.

Durkin knew exactly what Diana was referring to. She was pointing at the Rotherham Registry Office. She wanted him to marry her there and then. That way neither of them would have any time for regrets. It was all or nothing as far as both of them were concerned, or so Diana hoped.

PC Durkin stopped for a moment on the pavement outside the registry office. He wanted a few seconds to think about what most people consider the most momentous decision of their lives. He thought about them as a couple. They seemed pretty happy. The sex was outstanding. She was a good cook. She seemed besotted by him. What else could a man want out of marriage?

He turned and put his arms around her and kissed her full on the lips as that icy wind blew around their ankles.

"Come on then. Let's get it over and done with, lass."

The registrar was used to slightly more advance notice of a wedding than Diana and Pat were prepared to give him.

"But you need witnesses. I cannot marry you without witnesses."

Nothing would deter the vibrant couple.

PC Durkin dashed down the steps of the office and spotted two old ladies pulling shopping trollies behind them.

"Excuse me, ladies. Would you mind doing me a very big favour?"

Ten minutes later, Mr and Mrs Durkin emerged from the registry office, complete with wedding certificate and the sort of beaming smiles that usually say it all. It was the most romantic day of Diana's life.

She turned to her loving husband and quietly whispered in his ear: "Til death us do part..."

On the way home to Kilnhurst that November day of 1984, Diana truly hoped that marrying PC Durkin would mark a new step towards everlasting happiness. She put all those thoughts of sexual abuse behind her. After all, they had reverted to more traditional ways to excite each other in recent weeks, so she hoped all his sadistic pleasures were now a thing of the past.

Maybe it was an inbuilt naivety on her part, but she was convinced that now they were married he would change into a full-time loving, caring husband rather than the brutal punisher he had shown himself to be earlier in their relationship.

But there was something missing from that wedding ceremony that deeply troubled Diana — a photographer. That night, as they cuddled and kissed romantically on the sofa, at the home that now belonged to both of them, she stopped to ask him:

"What about some photos to mark the event?"

"You arrange it. We'll go to a studio and have them done really nicely."

Diana was so pleased now. She would have an everlasting memento of her dream marriage to the man of her fantasies.

"I'll wear an extra-special outfit just for the occasion."

She was already planning a very sexy surprise for the man in her life.

Wedding photographer Tony Munclark had thought he'd seen it all before when Diana and Pat Durkin came excitedly into his studio for a "very special photo session". She clutched her new husband's arm, just like they always did straight after a wedding. Sadly, that lovingness was, more often than not, soon forgotten in the midst of the long-term warfare that mostly passed for marriage.

But, for the moment, they looked like every happy couple Tony had ever photographed during his career. She had on a smart well-fitted white skirt and matching jacket that any bride would have been proud of. And PC Durkin wore his best dark suit with a white tie and shirt just to add that matrimonial feeling to the occasion.

As photographer Tony snapped happily away, he could see through his viewfinder that Diana Durkin was really getting a kick out of having her picture taken. She wrapped one leg around her new husband's hips. Then she twisted and squirmed her own legs together and licked her lips with the tip of her tongue as the shutter kept clicking away.

Every few moments she got more and more daring. Soon she was probing her husband's ear with her tongue, urging the slightly surprised photographer to "carry on — don't stop".

The truth was pretty obvious for PC Durkin and that photographer to see. She was getting very turned on by the photo session. But there was still more to come.

"Can you just stop for a second, please."

The photographer did not mind. He was being paid by the hour and, in any case, this was certainly turning out to be slightly more interesting than your average set of wedding pictures.

But even he was surprised when Diana unzipped her skirt before wriggling it down to the ground. Then she undid the buttons on her blouse and took that off as well.

Both men were stunned. But Diana was not finished yet. Now wearing just a smooth white basque, complete with garters and sheer white stockings, she yelled a command at the bewildered Tony:

"Right. Off you go — I want some really steamy pictures to remember this day by."

PC Pat Durkin was delighted, if a bit stunned, by his brand new wife's extraordinary display of exhibitionism. As she put both her arms around him and nudged her knee into his groin ever so gently, he could not help feeling sexually charged. He was definitely looking forward to getting home that night.

By doing that very public strip, she had convinced PC Durkin that she was game for anything — and in his language that meant a whole assortment of sexual perversions.

The truth was that Diana was always trying desperately to get attention. Her jackboots, her sexy outfits and her strip at the wedding photographer's were all signs of her neverending efforts to please him, to make him happy. But if she had realised that she was simply convincing him that she would perform any sexual act in the name of her love for him, then she would never have done any of those things in the first place.

Meanwhile, PC Durkin's sick and twisted mind was planning a new series of torments for his brand new bride . . .

Diana Durkin was petrified. Her husband had just wrapped a leather gag around her face and she was having trouble breathing. She kept thinking back to the wedding, the photographs, the happiness. Now, just a few hours after all that, she was being submitted to the sort of degrading act she thought she had married him to escape from.

PC Durkin's idea of sexual fun was to punish his partner in every way he could think of. Maybe it was all those years of working in the police force and keeping his cool in the face of so much danger that did it? Perhaps he had repressed his anger and hatred towards women for so long that it had to get out eventually?

Whatever the reason, Durkin was only concerned with one thing as he tied his wife's arms tightly behind her back — his own self-gratification. This was just the beginning of his sexual merry-go-round. He fully intended to take his wife to the edge of sadism at its very worst. And then he had other plans as well...

Diana Durkin was stifling the tears because she knew he would pull the ropes even tighter if he heard her crying. She just wished she had never married him. This was living hell and there was no way of escape.

As she felt his hands smashing across her head and back, she tried to console herself with the thought that perhaps she had brought it on herself. She would do anything for him within the normally acceptable bounds of sexual foreplay, but this was too horrible to contemplate.

When it was over, he untied the gag. It was covered in her saliva where she had bitten right through it in a vain bid to avoid the pain that was searing her body. He did not utter a word to her. It was just remotely possible that his own climax had left him feeling just a bit guilty for the outrageous acts he had committed. But, then again, his face showed no remorse.

Diana Durkin cried herself to sleep that night. Her mind was just a jumble of confusion. The emotional highs of the wedding had been completely destroyed by the sick and twisted acts he had performed on her. She needed time to think about the future. How was she going to escape?

The next day at work, even her colleagues noticed that she was not the same happy, vibrant, sexy Diana of old.

"That's what marriage does to you, Di," said one tactless work pal. If only he had known just how close to the truth he really was.

The only thing that remained the same about Diana that day were her clothes — she still wore her traditional black tight-fitting dress, but now she was not capable of flirting with the clients or showing off a little bit of thigh like before. He had destroyed all that. She would never openly display her sexuality again. He had punished her for being so uninhibited. She had learnt her lesson.

Diana dreaded getting home each night in the days following the wedding. Her husband — the man whom she had thought she loved enough to marry less than a week earlier — had become a morose monster whose only conversation consisted of orders like:

"Take your clothes off."

"Bend over."

"Do as I tell you."

She kept wishing she had never worn those Nazi jackboots or the other sexy outfits, then he might not have presumed he could abuse her the way he was now intent on doing each and every evening.

But PC Pat Durkin felt no guilt. Every day at work he let his mind wander to what he had planned for that evening's "entertainment" with his wife. Like a heroin addict looking for a bigger and bigger fix, PC Durkin needed to make each act even more outrageous than the one before. Hours of his working day were taken up with thinking them through. Planning them down to the last intricate detail. That was part of the thrill for him. In fact, he felt almost as excited when he thought through his sadistic pleasures as when it all actually happened.

Yet Diana Durkin somehow persevered with her husband. Something inside her made her believe that she could mend their relationship. There was still hope, despite the pain and suffering.

That eternal optimism was part of her character. It was the same ingredient that had created a bubbly, extrovert persona that PC Durkin had mistaken for a love of perverted sex.

But on the fifth night of their married life together,

the sick and twisted mind of the deviant bobby took on a whole new dimension. Not even the ever-tolerant Diana could stand the thought of what her husband proposed.

She looked down at the growling Alsatian and refused point-blank to move until he had taken the animal out of their bedroom. It was at that point she knew that her marriage had truly been made in hell.

The following evening, conversation between husband and wife was virtually non-existent. PC Durkin was still sulking from what he saw as her refusal to co-operate in his sickly bid for sexual gratification.

Diana Durkin was too afraid to talk to him in case he beat her, as he had done pretty regularly in the past. She kept asking herself why she had even married this monster who hid behind the veneer of respectability through his career as a policeman.

As she watched him pour himself his seventh glass of straight whisky that night, she wondered how much longer she could live in that awful place.

"I'm goin' to bed."

She prayed that he would not follow. She somehow hoped he would stay behind in the kitchen and drink himself into oblivion before collapsing on the sofa. But that was purely wishful thinking on her part.

Within minutes of her pulling the covers tightly over herself he appeared, swaying with the drink and blowing booze-sodden fumes all around the room. She tried to pull the blanket even closer but he yanked it away viciously. She lay there, exposed to his drunken eyes, like a pervert's feast laid out and ready to eat.

She knew this time she would not be able to take any more of his abuse. Her tolerance level was at an all-time low. She shut her eyes tightly and prayed that sleep would take over before anything more could occur.

"Get out, you bitch. Get out."

Diana did not move at first. She was scared she might incite him further so she lay like a stone on the bed.

"You heard me. Get out."

She wished that she could just fall asleep. Even her worst nightmares were not as bad as the reality she faced that evening. But PC Durkin had not finished.

She sensed him lunging towards her, so she moved out of the bed speedily and wrapped a dressing gown around herself. She looked around to see his drunken body collapsed on the bed, so she headed towards the kitchen to wait a few minutes for him to be safely asleep.

By the time she crept back into the bedroom he looked truly sound asleep. She lay down on the edge of the bed and pulled the covers over herself very gently so as not to disturb the monster.

It must have been way past midnight by the time she actually got to sleep. Her dreams were just as pleasant as she had hoped for.

"Come on, bitch. Do it."

Dawn was just peeping through the curtains when Diana opened her eyes to that familiar aggressive tone she had come to loathe so much. Her husband — the gentle policeman so adored by the community — was trying to molest her as she lay next to him. She pushed him away roughly, but regretted it almost immediately.

She should have known better. He never slept past dawn when he had been drinking heavily. Why on earth did she return to that bed in the first place? Maybe she just thought there was a small chance she might wake up the next morning and he would be a changed man. The truth was that he would never change.

"Get out then."

PC Durkin gave his bride of just seven days two choices.

105

"If you don't want to do it, get out. Why d'you come back in here in the first place?"

Diana Durkin clenched her fists with anger. The fear she usually felt had been replaced by a deep-set fury. She had taken just about enough. She got up from the bed and headed for the wardrobe in silence.

PC Durkin was still in an alcoholic haze and took little notice of her as she searched through the wardrobe for something. He just taunted her over and over.

"You're useless. I don't know why I even married you. You're only good for one thing."

If he had bothered to look up at that moment, he might have seen the German Luger pointing straight at him. She wished he would watch her, then he would see the end just before it came. That would make the killing even more satisfying. She wanted him to know it was her, then he might realise why.

But PC Pat Durkin lay there as if he did not have a care in the world. All his cruelty to his first wife and now his second was about to catch up with him in a deadly fashion.

She pointed the gun towards his head and squeezed as tight as she could. The muscles on her index finger strained with the tension, but there was nothing she could do to stop it now. The gun jerked downwards slightly in her hand.

The bullet entered his throat and pierced a one-inch hole right through his neck. It was enough to end his abuse for ever.

Next door, neighbour Ferenc Pinter had just got up, when he heard a noise like nothing else he had ever experienced in his lifetime.

"I heard a cry, a death cry. Then all went quiet."

In July, 1985, Diana Durkin was put on probation for three years for killing her 36-year-old husband. Her plea of guilty to manslaughter on the grounds of provocation and diminished responsibility was accepted by the judge Mr Justice Hodgson, at Sheffield Crown Court.

The judge told the court: "She poses no danger to anyone," and he also said she had been subjected to "sadistic behaviour" over a long period.

One of the conditions of Diana Durkin's probation was that she become an in-patient at a psychiatric hospital in Bradford, Yorkshire. PC Durkin's first wife Jenny is believed to still be a psychiatric patient in another mental home.

7
I Hate "It"

The Modin farmyard was like something out of another century. The rundown main house looked as if a group of hillbillies had long since abandoned it to the ravages of wild animals. Many of the windows were broken or simply non-existent, their frames hanging limply from hinges, primed for firewood and little else. Step on the porch and your foot would likely plunge through rotten wood. The roof, too, had seen better days. Its flimsy tiles had been ripped off in the furious storms that tumbled down the mountains and across the plains every winter.

Dogs and horses roamed freely in and out of the house and all the surrounding barns as if they owned the place. Every now and again a dog would rummage through the piles of rotting rubbish that leant against the outhouses. The starving animals would devour anything that might pass as food — some decaying piece of fly-infested meat perhaps, or an old tin that might have just a morsel still in it.

The place was covered in shit. Hundreds and hundreds of piles, dotted around the yard like little ant hills. They had long since turned hard in the summer heat but it was difficult to avoid stepping on them as you tried to make your way across the yard to the main house.

To an outsider the Modin farm really did look like the ultimate Orwellian nightmare. A dilapidated, uninhabited place that had long since been deserted by humans. The locals even nicknamed it "Animal Farm". It was only the sign at the rotting gate that gave any clue to the fact that somehow one human being still lived there:

STALLIONS AND GUARD DOGS, PLEASE STAY

IN THE CAR. IF AT HOME, WE WILL COME TO GATE. THANKS.

Betty Modin was determined to cut herself off from the outside world as much as possible. The animals were her protectors now. She talked to them. Fed them (when she had the funds) and loved them in her own strange way.

In fact, she looked like a wild animal herself. Her thick grey hair, matted in clumps that stuck to her scalp and clothes, which couldn't have been washed since they were bought, made it quite clear where her priorities lay. Fashion had long since passed her by. But then, at 60 years of age, she had no interest in anything other than her dearly beloved animals. She often used to say that in a perfect world she would never have to speak to a human again as long as she lived.

Some believed she was driven into her bizarre life in the Canadian wilderness by the pain and anguish of an unhappy marriage. It had closed her off, until she had secured for herself a private world of her own which she could cope with. In order to survive, however, she had to put up with the very man she hated and despised so much — her husband Norman.

In 1977 they had finally agreed to separate. Norman could no longer stand her temper tantrums and her weird ideals. She had taken little interest in the upbringing of their children. She rarely spoke to them kindly. Instead, she would shout and rant at Norman and then retreat into her little imaginary world where humans played but a tiny role.

Yet the most vivid memory Betty Modin's children had of their mother was when she brutally killed some of the very animals she adored so much. One of her daughters never forgot how Betty made her tie a dog to a fence and then shot the animal in cold blood because it had killed two ducks. She'd done it there and then, in front of a girl who was only 11 at the time. It was a memory that would haunt the daughter for the rest of her life.

When Betty and Norman split up it was a relief for the whole family. Gentle Norman could not wait to get away from his selfish wife and start a new life on the other side of the country. But he still accepted that he would have to provide for Betty and promised to pay her $1,100 a month to keep herself and her animals in the manner to which they had become accustomed.

But the marriage break-up simply provided Betty with the perfect opportunity to escape from reality for ever. With just enough cash each month to keep things going single-handedly, she sank into a timeless existence. Just so long as that cheque came through the post each month, she could keep her animals — and that was all that counted. Her dog-food bill alone came to $500 a month. That was, when she remembered to buy it. But then Betty did not care about the state of the farm. Her life was now so interlocked with her darlings that their survival meant her survival. Who cared about bricks and mortar?

When, on October 6, 1981, husband Norman turned up for a rare visit to the Canadian wilderness, Betty was not exactly surprised. She had sensed a note of edginess in her estranged husband recently when they spoke on the phone or exchanged letters. She genuinely feared that his visit might have been prompted by a decision to cut off the monthly payments that made her strange lifestyle possible.

Betty may have preferred the company of animals, but she was still a quick-witted, intelligent woman when she wanted to be. In fact, it was her razor-sharp perception of life that probably made her such a loner. She neither trusted nor particularly liked human beings — it was as simple as that.

And now the man she had referred to as "it" for most of their married life was making a highly suspicious visit to her rundown home. She knew "it" was hardly likely to be making the long trek to profess his love for her. Love was just a distant memory. Betty wasn't sure whether it had ever existed at all.

Though 61, Norman Modin had enjoyed a whole new lease of life the moment he had left Betty. It took their separation for him to realise just how much of life he had missed out on. His new world consisted of a responsible job as an aircraft mechanic and a comfortable home in the picturesque town of Fort Nelson in British Columbia.

The last thing he wanted to do was visit the rotting ruin of a house that Betty clung to. He had been dreading the journey for weeks, but he steeled himself. It had to be done. It was high time they discussed the money he had willingly been shelling out for the previous four years. Now all the kids were grown up, he believed it was right to divorce and cut down on those crippling payments that were biting into his monthly salary.

As Norman arrived at the huge Edmonton International Airport, he promised himself it would be as brief a visit as possible. He truly hated staying at the farm. She had allowed it to become such a dreadful, unhygienic place that he had refused to sleep in the main farmhouse on the previous couple of visits. Now, he came well prepared for a cold, but relatively clean night sleeping in his hire-car in one of the outhouses.

It was for that reason he had chosen a 1980 blue and grey Mercury Lynx rental as his cosy home for the next twenty-four hours. At least the pristine vehicle with its comfortable cloth interior would provide him with some escape from the disgusting place his wife called home.

As Norman Modin drove the two-hour journey to his wife's residence, he tuned in the radio to a news station and listened intently to the shock event of that day — the assassination of Egyptian president Anwar Sadat. It was a momentous time in Middle Eastern politics, and many feared that the death of the peace-loving statesman might spark a bloody conflict in the world's most volatile region. US warships stood by nervously, Israel's sabre rattled and the world took a deep breath.

Norman Modin probably felt just as concerned as millions of other North Americans as he journeyed across the barren flatlands. But October 6, 1981 was going to end up being the most significant date in his life for an entirely different reason.

"Betty. We must talk."

Betty Modin knew the moment she heard the tone of her husband's voice that trouble was brewing. They might have loathed each other for much of their married life together, but she still knew Norman inside out. That was one of the reasons she grew so contemptuous of him. She could always tell what he was going to say before he even got halfway through his stumbling sentences. As far as she was concerned, he was an old bore and the less she had to talk to him the better.

As she sat in the dusty armchair that had once been the family's pride and joy, she considered how to solve the problem at hand. Her husband sat opposite her in another seat that had been badly ravaged by some of the ill-trained dogs that were constantly flowing through that front room like an army of protectors around the short-tempered, eccentric Betty.

"I cannot afford to keep paying you all this money each month."

Norman was nervous about telling her. He had been dreading this moment for weeks, but at least he was finally tackling the situation head on.

Betty did not reply. She just looked at him through glasses that were perched on the end of her beak-like nose.

"Well. How much can we cut it down to, Betty?"
Norman had started, so he was not about to retreat. It had to be done. He had to sort it all out.

But Betty's mind was working overtime. She was infuriated. Yet again her husband had proved to be such a bloody predictable bastard. How dare he try and cut off her money? Without it the animals would starve. She did not care about herself, but they were her pride and joy and no-one was going to take her "children" from her.

Betty was not even going to allow him the pleasure of a reply. She reckoned there were other ways to ensure the money continued flowing through.

Norman Modin was concerned by Betty's apparently meek acceptance. He took her refusal to talk about it as an agreement that he should cut down the monthly payments considerably. He continued on his mission:

"How about $500 a month? Surely that would see you through pretty comfortably?"

Still Betty sat there in silence. Why should she degrade herself by even commenting on his outrageous proposition? He never did care anything about the animals she had so cherished. Years earlier he had given her the choice: save her marriage or stay with the animals. Betty Modin said she had no choice at that time, and it was the same now as they tried to "talk things through". How could he sit there in her house, watching all her little "children" playing in the living room, without realising that nothing would persuade her to sacrifice the ones she loved?

Outside, a horse galloped past the window. Betty Modin decided there and then that nothing would get in her way.

Norman Modin left her, without getting a reply, and trotted off to the barn where his rental car and sleeping bag awaited him. So she wouldn't speak? Let the old bat have her moment of glory. At least he had told her. She couldn't claim later that he had not

113

given her a chance to air her opinions.

The night air was silent for once. So deathly quiet that the only noise was the distant patter of some of the dogs walking across the yard. Then, in the distance, the whirr of a single-prop aircraft — probably a farmer late home from an errand — flying across the canyon a few miles to the east.

On the porch, at least twenty dogs slept peacefully. Every now and again one of them would scratch its stomach as a fat, sleepy fruit-fly landed on its coat. Away from the house, the darkness was complete. No shadows. No figures. No light. Just a sea of black permeating the entire countryside. The barn where Norman Modin snored in his rental car was just a few yards away from the main house. He felt quite safe and snug there — it was certainly an improvement on the flea-infested mattresses that he had once suffered in the name of marital bliss.

When the huge, high door to that barn slowly creaked open, Norman was already at peace with the world. Probably dreaming about some distant paradise where there were no dogs, no horses and no Betty Modin. He did not even stir when some of the dogs followed the old woman in. Outside, a gentle breeze had picked up over the barren pastures. It rustled around Betty Modin's ankles for a few moments as she crept slowly and silently over the straw-covered floor. The pitter-patter of her dogs' paws on the same surface sounded like rain coming through the gaping holes in the roof.

A beacon of light suddenly appeared as Betty Modin switched on her small hand-torch and shone it down on the ground before panning it up to the door handle of the Mercury Lynx. She stood there for a moment, thinking. Then one of her dogs rubbed itself against her leg and she remembered why she was there. They were more important to her than anything else in the world. No-one was going to take them away.

114

A slight smile came to her lips as she examined the car door by torchlight. It was unlocked. Perfect.

She stood absolutely still for a moment and waited again. Then she heard it. A slow, sniffling snore. She did not want to shine her torch right in at him until the last possible moment, but she had to make sure he was asleep. For the first time in her life, that snoring sound was reassuring. She had endured so many years of his snoring sleeping habits with a faint disgust. But now she was delighted he made so much noise because it was encouraging her to prepare for a triumphant moment in her life.

Her hand grasped the door handle tightly and she clicked it up. It was such a modern model that the door opened with ease. Her torchlight still shone on the floor, guiding her. She cast the beam across his shoes protruding from the bottom of his sleeping bag. He looked snug covered up like that. For a split second she let the light wander over his craggy face. She would not miss him.

Now was the time. Now he would pay the price for trying to destroy her little kingdom at "Animal Farm".

Betty Modin had handled guns since she was eleven years old, so she did not exactly struggle with the shotgun in her right hand. Standing in a cold, precise stance, she held the wooden end tight against her shoulder blade and aimed at his body, still sleeping soundly just two feet away.

The blast of shot sounded more like a loud thud than a gun firing. The 250-odd pieces of shot pierced that quilted sleeping bag like a rainstorm of metal fragments. Betty watched as he came to — in shock. She shone her torch right in his eyes. She wanted to see the fear in his eyes. He tried to move, in a desperate bid to stop her firing any further shots. But his thigh had been torn to shreds by the force of the blast. In any case, Betty Modin had no intention of firing any more. She wanted to leave him to die a slow and anguished death. He was not going to enjoy the luxury of a quick, sudden execution. In her mind, he deserved the worst type of punishment imaginable.

Three of her dogs leapt up and started to sniff and lick at the gaping wound. One of them chomped up a tattered piece of flesh lying beside him. A good meal. And there might be more yet. Betty left without a word, calling the dogs away as if she were out on a quiet walk in the countryside.

She felt no remorse. Just relief that she had finally done it. The payments would continue on his standing order. She had already decided that as far as the rest of the world was concerned, her husband had disappeared without trace. By morning he would be no more.

Norman Modin fell into a deep coma within seconds of his wife leaving the dingy barn. He was losing blood at an alarming rate and he simply could not fight the fatigue that had overwhelmed his body. He never recovered consciousness and, about two hours later, he died through loss of blood.

The next day, Betty did not even bother to go into the barn to see whether her dying husband had somehow managed to crawl out of his crypt. She knew he would be going no place ever again.

She got out a hammer and some splintered wood from across the yard and nailed the doors closed. She had no intention of ever going into that outhouse again. She had achieved what she set out to do — and that was all that mattered.

As the weeks passed and the police came and went, Betty staved off everyone with great skill. She got to quite enjoy telling her story of how her husband never actually turned up to see her on that day in October as he had promised.

She said it was typical of her hard-drinking, estranged, bully of a husband. She reckoned he had probably headed down to Los Angeles.

"It's the sort of place he would like because he is

116

one of "those'." She said it in such whispered tones that the policeman interviewing her did not have the faintest idea what she was on about at first.

"Excuse me, Mrs Modin, but what is one of "those'?"

"You know," she hesitated for a moment. It hurt her even to refer to them by name. "A homosexual."

The cop nodded his head understandingly. He would have dearly loved to put her story to the test by searching every inch of that disgusting flea-ridden, rundown farm. There was something about her that he did not trust. Maybe it was the cold stare or the unemotional response each time he talked to her about her recently departed husband.

But there was no actual evidence to link Betty Modin to her husband's mysterious disappearance. Not a shred of proof that she was the person who might be responsible for his vanishing act. For that reason the officer could not even obtain a search warrant to turn the place upside down.

Just a few feet away, the corpse of Norman Modin was gradually being devoured by the insects and rodents that had inhabited that barn for far longer than him.

Betty Modin tried not to give her husband much thought after the dust settled and the inquiries as to his whereabouts ceased. She was just delighted to be able to get on with her sole ambition in life — to raise her "children" in a safe, happy environment. As the months passed, she continued receiving her husband's cheques — thanks to his standing order and the blank cheques she took from the case he had left in the living room before his death. Betty would forge his signature and then send them to his bank account in British Columbia so that the account he set up for her would continue to be healthy for some years to come. Luckily for her, Norman had been a good saver and, at the rate of $1,100 a month, she knew he had sufficient funds to keep her going well into old age.

And, for some unknown reason, the police investigating the disappearance of Norman Modin never thought to check his bank accounts until many years later.

Over the next few years, Betty never once felt tempted to look inside that barn at the once-gleaming car which her husband had hired. If she had, she would have seen that the cruel, harsh winters had proven beyond doubt that the ability of the Mercury to resist long-term rusting was non-existent. But that was hardly her concern. She was more preoccupied with running the farm and keeping all those animals happy.

Her two daughters were shocked, but hardly surprised, when they occasionally visited their mother. The buildings were getting even more rundown and the plastic rubbish bags were now piled high against a wall around the back of that very same barn where her husband lay entombed. Many of the bags had gashes in them where the dogs had ripped them open in a desperate bid to find a source of food.

Yet her daughters found her as mentally alert as ever. It was as if the disgusting state of her home was completely unrelated to her ability to think and act quickly. Her clothes may have been drab and filthy but her mind was sharp.

One day she held a completely coherent, topical conversation with one of her daughters for two hours on the subject of American politics. She hardly ever read a newspaper and only occasionally listened to the radio, but she seemed to know everything that was going on.

"Bush is just not strong enough. He needs more edge."

Her daughter looked around at the filthy hovel her mother called home and wondered how on earth she had ever survived such an eccentric upbringing. She thanked God she had managed to escape.

Almost nine years later — in September, 1990 — police sergeants Del Huget and Joseph Zubkowski decided they would re-open the file on missing Norman Modin and do one last bit of detective work to see if they could solve the disappearance that had troubled a good few of their predecessors.

When they uncovered the fact that no-one had bothered to investigate Norman Modin's financial status, they started one last digging operation and soon discovered that someone had been forging cheques in his name and that Betty Modin was still receiving her monthly payments.

Once again the finger of suspicion pointed at Betty, now a spritely 70-year-old. But those forged cheques were not enough evidence in themselves to persuade a judge to issue a search warrant. So officers Huget and Zubkowski decided to pay the eccentric lady a visit.

Betty Modin was a bit taken aback when the two policemen called at her home on September 4, 1990. It had been many years since her last visit from the law and she had actually presumed that the whole matter was now dead and buried.

The officers seemed friendly enough, but she was very concerned as to why they should come back to her after such a long time. Betty repeated her allegations that Norman Modin was a homosexual who had probably fled to Los Angeles, and tried to cut short the two detectives' visit by claiming she had to feed the horses.

But before she could persuade them to leave they asked her one last question.

"When was the last day you saw your husband, Mrs Modin?"

A long period of time had elapsed since the last time she had been asked that question by the police. She hesitated. Then it came to her.

"It was the day of Anwar Sadat's assassination. I

119

remember hearing it on the radio."

The officers shook their heads and made a note of Betty Modin's reply without even realising the significance of it. They departed for Edmonton just a few minutes later, none the wiser in the mystery of Norman Modin's disappearance.

Back at the police precinct, Huget and Zubkowski were just going through the motions of putting the case to bed for ever, when Huget checked through Betty Modin's original statement to police back in 1981.

Then he spotted it. Betty had clearly claimed that she never even saw her husband on that fateful day of the Sadat killing. She had always stuck steadfastly to her story that he had never shown up to stay at the farm that day. Now, the police had evidence that she was lying. It was enough to get an immediate search warrant issued and within hours they had returned to the filthy farmhouse that was home to countless animals and the very weird Betty Modin.

The huge doors of that barn took quite an effort to open. But, thanks mainly to a thick metal jack, the two officers managed to prise them apart after a few minutes.

Betty Modin stood on the porch as they forced their way in. Huget and Zubkowski panned their eyes around the dusty, insect-filled air, which was illuminated by the strong sunlight penetrating every corner of the barn. The unmistakably poignant stench of decaying flesh overwhelmed them.

The two men looked at each other for a moment and then headed towards the rusting remains of the Mercury. The car was covered in a tapestry of cobwebs broken only by the infestation of maggots and mouse droppings that adorned much of the bodywork.

Huget glanced down at the mice scurrying away from the underneath of the car and gasped as a sweet, sickly odour threatened to gag him. It hung

120

thick in the air and caught in his throat so that he had to swallow to avoid choking. He found himself clearing his throat again and again.

His partner Zubkowski stood back in silence. Both men knew what they were about to find but they were trying to delay the awful moment for as long as possible.

Huget gingerly opened the door. Trying to avoid the crust of insects, he pulled carefully at the handle. But it did not move. He was dreading the moment, but unless he actually pulled that door open with some real force it would not budge. Ten years of inactivity had done more than just rust a few hinges.

He drew a deep breath and pulled with all his strength. The door eased open slowly and there, on the back seat was the partial mummified body of Norman Modin. They had built themselves up into such a state of anxious expectation that the reality of the situation was not quite so horrendous. It looked more like something from a horror movie set than an actual corpse.

At first, they both tried to avoid looking at his face. Their eyes started at his feet, still covered in the leather shoes he had put on for that last fateful journey from his home in British Columbia. They were peeping out rigidly from the bottom of the sleeping bag — almost as if they were unconnected to the grotesque head that slumped limply to one side, with a yellow cap perched precariously at an angle.

One side of the face had been eaten down to the bone by the armies of termites that had feasted on his remains for ten long years. But the other side of his face was still remarkably intact because he had slumped against the side of the sleeping bag and the insects had not been able to penetrate that part of his head.

Huget and Zubkowski both swallowed hard as they examined the remains of Norman Modin in absolute silence. Suddenly, Huget felt something wet and moist at his ankle. He was startled and jumped back a few inches before realising that one of Betty Modin's dogs was sniffing at his feet. Then another three came barging into the barn and tried to break past the two policemen blocking the way to the car.

The dogs were like hungry savages, having smelt the congealed and rotting remains of the man who was once their master. Huget and Zubkowski struggled to hold back the dogs and slammed the car door shut to stop them getting to the corpse.

Out on the porch, Betty Modin felt relieved. That dark and disturbing secret had remained locked inside her mind for longer than any human could be expected to tolerate. Now, at least, the fear of her husband being discovered was no more.

But her only concern as the two detectives read Betty Modin her rights was her animals. She knew they would never survive without all her loving care and attention.

On December 6, 1991, Betty Modin stood emotionless as Justice Alex Murray found her guilty of the manslaughter of her husband. Six weeks later, the 71-year-old widow was sentenced to four years in jail after the same judge told her: "I consider the degree of culpability on your part to be of a high order. In fixing sentence, this court must consider the fact that such behaviour is unacceptable and therefore repudiated by society."

Modin was also ordered never to touch any firearm again. Justice Murray also ordered that her term 'be served in a facility near Edmonton where medical service was readily available as her health had seriously declined after her arrest and she was in need of a hip replacement operation, as well as suffering from severe arthritis.

8

Deadly Revenge

"Just do it for me, honey."

It was as a result of those immortal words that Maxine O'Neill allowed herself to become the rather unpleasant object of her husband's sick sexual desires.

They'd both worked late at the bar they owned, when the ever-so-drunk Jerry O'Neill had come up with an outrageous bedtime plan for that night. He wanted his attractive brunette wife to have sex with another man while he watched. Then he intended to make her watch him doing it with the stranger.

The depressing thing was that 46-six-year-old Maxine was not in the least bit surprised by her husband's sordid sexual appetites. She had long suspected he was bisexual. But, as is so often the case in marriages across the globe, she could not actually confront him with her suspicions. Instead, she kept them bottled up, afraid that if she started accusing him then he would turn on her and beat her, like he usually did for the slightest reasons.

Jerry O'Neill had already chatted up a man in the bar earlier. He had arranged for the stranger to come back at closing time so that the "happy" threesome could head off to the O'Neill farm in Pike County, Arkansas. He did not even consider his wife's feelings in the matter. He certainly did not expect her to object. On the contrary, Jerry O'Neill reckoned his wife would have a ball in bed with two men. He could not have been more wrong.

Maxine was very worried. By suggesting the *ménage à trois*, her 44-year-old husband had finally confirmed her deepest suspicions. Now she had to face the emotional upheaval of discovering her husband was bisexual — and being forced into a sexual scenario she most certainly did not want to act out.

"I won't do it, Jerry. It's sick."

123

Maxine could not believe she had actually had the courage to tell him, but she had. Now she had to face the full wrath of her husband. He considered her opinions to be irrelevant. He certainly was not going to take no for an answer.

"It'll be fun."

There was no way that Jerry O'Neill was about to change his masterplan for a perverted orgy. She had no choice in the matter as far as he was concerned.

Then she saw him walk in the bar just as they were locking up. Maxine froze in her tracks and looked at him. She turned her eyes away the moment she caught his gaze. The last thing she wanted to do was encourage this stranger — this man who was expecting to share her with Jerry.

She could feel his eyes panning across her body. Looking at her legs, her breasts. But there was little or no interest in her face. If he had bothered to examine her, he would have seen pretty features framed by thick, shoulder-length brown hair. Lips loosely parted. A neat nose. But this wasn't about people being attracted to each other. This was the preliminary round in the build-up to a sexual threesome that was filling Maxine with equal amounts of fear and loathing.

They sat in silence on the ten-mile journey back to the O'Neill farm. With Jerry at the wheel, Maxine was jammed between the two men on the bench seat in the front of the pick-up. She pointed out that she would prefer to sit out in the open on the back. But Jerry gave her one of those evil looks that she had seen so many times before, so she agreed to sit sandwiched between the two men who planned to have sex with her.

Every time the other man's knee touched her, she blanched and went rigid. There was no way she was going to encourage the inevitable. Even when Jerry pulled her towards him and French kissed her as they waited at a set of traffic lights, she did not respond.

124

She felt his rough tongue probing deeply into the back of her mouth. Her husband smelt of whiskey, and lots of it. But he didn't care. He was just showing off in front of his new best friend.

When they untangled after that lingering kiss, Jerry O'Neill turned to the stranger sitting next to them and winked. It was an unsubtle gesture, deliberately designed to intimidate his wife into realising that there was no escape from what he had planned. Maxine tried to nuzzle close to her husband even though she hated him for what he was about to put her through. She reckoned that at least the other guy might get the message and have second thoughts after seeing she was so obviously not interested. But all it really did was make Jerry believe that she was more than happy to have sex with both of them.

By the time they rolled up at the farmhouse, Maxine was resigned to her fate. She did not have the strength to fight them. He had won yet again. She shut her eyes tightly and thought about the rest of her miserable life, while a hand moved up her leg. Then another hand moved over her breasts. It was only the beginning of a night of sexual torture. Jerry O'Neill and his friend had bigger, bolder plans for their sex-slave Maxine.

By the time Maxine finally got to sleep, she could feel virtually every bone in her body ache. Her insides felt as if they had been ripped to shreds. She had endured hours and hours of sexual molestation, all in the good name of marriage. Every orifice in her body had been penetrated. She turned away from her slumbering husband and his new best friend and sobbed into the pillow. This was truly a marriage made in hell.

The next morning, Maxine woke up good and early and slipped out of the house before she had to face either her husband or the man he had encouraged to rape her the previous evening.

She had work to attend to on the farm they owned. It also gave her the perfect excuse to talk to the two labourers they employed as helpers on the luscious green spread of Arkansas countryside.

Harold Hamlin and Paul Jenkins were nothing like her husband. They were hard-working hired hands who spoke few words but had a philosophical outlook on life. They had both seen a lot of the world — good and bad — and would no doubt move on to fresh pastures within a few months.

But at least they offered Maxine an ear to listen to her woes. They were the only two people she could speak candidly to about her husband's activities. Naturally, she did not go into explicit detail. She did not need to. The two men lived on the farm and they knew perfectly well what was going on.

Maxine had grown particularly fond of Paul Jenkins. He was a tall, sinewy man with a drooping moustache that made him look like a character from *Bonanza*. He felt really sorry for Maxine. It seemed so unfair that a woman of such kindness, such vitality should end up this way. He could not understand why she put up with so much.

"I got no choice. If I left I'd have nothing."

That was her stock reply every time Paul tried to suggest that she would be better off out of the farm and her husband's life. He found it particularly frustrating because he was growing increasingly fond of this vulnerable woman.

Sometimes he would find himself alone with her in one of the outhouses and he would feel the urge to grab hold of her and kiss her. To start with, he did not have the courage to do it. He was afraid she might take offence, and that would cost him his job. But eventually they would grow so close it would not matter.

And Maxine was definitely becoming aware of Paul's interest in her. It flattered her. It made her feel wanted. It also took her mind off that awful marriage to Jerry.

"I'm gonna do it. I can't take any more of him. It's the only way."

As Maxine's relationship with Paul Jenkins developed, so did her out and out hatred for her husband. She was at last beginning to see the light. All those years of drunken sexual perversion had finally taken their toll on her. Every time she saw Jerry she felt sick in the stomach. He physically disgusted her now. She kept asking herself: How could I ever have loved this man?

For his part, Jerry O'Neill was pickling his liver in alcohol so constantly that he had already sentenced himself to death from cirrhosis of the liver within a year at the most. But a year was much too long for Maxine to wait. The build up of hatred for her husband had reached boiling point — and it was about to manifest itself in a grisly act of murder.

Jerry O'Neill was slumped in bed still fully dressed when Maxine saw her first chance. He had got so drunk the previous evening that he could not even manage to remove his shoes before falling on top of the duvet.

She prodded him hard with her finger to see if there was any response. Nothing. Not even a change in his breathing pattern. He was dead to the world. She wished he was dead outright, then it would make her life much easier. But he had passed out from over-drinking, nothing more. However, he had presented her with an opportunity to escape from his sick and twisted ways.

Ever so quietly she crept to the bathroom and opened the medicine cupboard. Inside was a huge syringe already filled with what looked like blood. But it was all bubbly. None of the air had been gently pressed out. It looked like a strange concoction. Maxine hoped it would prove to be a lethal cocktail. In fact she had painstakingly prepared it the previous day. First she took the blood from one of the many chickens in the farmyard. Then she deliberately "gassed it up" with air bubbles, just to make sure it would cause maximum damage.

Now she was standing over her husband with this massive syringe, hopefully about to sentence him to a very painful death. She leant down over him, wondering where was the best place to insert the needle. She had to be fast. If he woke halfway through, she knew he would probably explode with anger and then she would be the one looking death in the eye.

After a few hesitant moments, she plunged the syringe into his stomach. It just seemed the biggest area, so she reckoned she could not fail. As she pressed the syringe down hard with her thumb she could feel the rumbling of the bubbles of air blocking the rush of the chicken blood into his system. But she just kept pressing hard, determined to empty every last drop into his body.

Jerry O'Neill did not stir an inch. Whatever he was dreaming about, it must have been good. A warm smile came over his lips halfway through Maxine's desperate bid to murder him. Jerry O'Neill obviously knew something she did not.

Maxine pulled the syringe out with a slight jolt and took it to the rubbish bin in the kitchen. Then she wandered back and, ever so casually, peeked down at her husband still lying there in a different world. That smile was still on his face. There was no sign of the mask of death contorting itself around his features. She could even hear his snoring getting irritatingly louder and louder. It was almost as if he was telling her she had failed. He was mocking her in his sleep. Maxine was very irritated. She stomped out of the bedroom and decided not to return for a few hours. Maybe it would take that long for the chicken blood and air bubbles to clog his system up for ever. Anyhow, she could not just stand there looking down at his pathetic heap of a body waiting for him to die. It would be much better if she returned later.

But when Maxine peeked in at her hubby after a few hours had passed, the only thing that had changed was his snoring. It was even louder than earlier. She would have to think up another way to get rid of him.

"Honey, this coffee tastes real good. Just what the doctor ordered."

Maxine looked over at her husband at the breakfast table and couldn't help watching him take another sip of that piping hot drink. This time it might actually work. She was lucky that all those years of heavy drinking had completely destroyed his tastebuds. Basically, he couldn't have tasted whether his food and drink was laced with rat poison. Strangely enough, that was yet another substance — together with crushed sleeping tablets — which Maxine O'Neill mixed in at every opportunity.

After more than a week of feeding the man a staple diet of enough poison and sleeping tablets to send a herd of elephants to heaven, Maxine finally began to see some hopeful signs. Jerry O'Neill kept slurring his words — even before he'd had his first drink of the morning. He kept stumbling over things. And, best of all, he was falling asleep in the most unlikely places — he seemed to have a particular fondness for choosing the toilet.

Maxine prayed that he might do the dirty deed to himself by falling asleep at the wheel of his truck. But he tended to avoid driving whenever he could, so it was unlikely.

Then it happened. One morning Jerry O'Neill literally could not get out of bed. At last, the poison had done its work.

"I can't get up, honey. I think I'm sick."

She couldn't resist allowing herself one long snigger in the kitchen as she made him a coffee, laced with yet more sleeping tablets. No point in wasting them. Still half a bottle left.

For two long weeks, she pretended to nurse her

bedridden husband while feeding him more and more poison. But he still hung on. Maxine was starting to lose her cool.

"When the hell is he goin' to die?"

She surprised her friend Paul Jenkins with her frankness. For the first time, she was admitting she had sentenced her husband to death. And Paul sympathised with her. After all, she had put up with more abuse and sick sexual desires than any woman could be expected to tolerate.

"Well. Let's kill him then."

He felt no doubt about the task that lay ahead. In any case, Paul Jenkins was by now so fond of Maxine that he wanted to spend the rest of his life with her. And all the cash they could get from selling the farm and the bar was an attractive proposition — kill off Jerry O'Neill and collect on his wife and his property.

October 10, 1989 seemed like a pretty ordinary working day on the farm. The grey skies opened up with heavy rainfall about breakfast time as labourers Harold Hamlin and Paul Jenkins toiled hard in the outhouses, organising the cattle.

Inside the main house, Maxine was still "nursing" her sickly husband. Desperately counting the minutes through the day in the hope that nightfall would come as quickly as possible.

Through the morning and afternoon, she had found herself pacing the hallway outside the bedroom in expectation of what was to come. She could not wait for it to happen.

It was Harold Hamlin who heard the gunshot. Just one single sound. No follow up. Just an eerie silence following the bang that came from the direction of the main house. For a few moments, he stood there wondering what to do. Then he looked towards the house and ran for the front door to investigate.

130

Inside the house, Hamlin found himself facing his workmate Paul Jenkins walking down the hallway with a pistol in his hand. They said nothing. But they both knew precisely what had happened. No words were needed.

Hamlin headed straight for the main bedroom. The sight that greeted him was horrendous. Jerry O'Neill, the heavy-set sex pervert who had dominated everyone throughout his life, was now quivering in the throes of death. A huge, gaping bullet wound in his head. Blood gushing down his face in torrents. His mouth contorted in shock and agony. His eyelids just managing to flicker during the last few moments of life.

Hamlin stared down at his boss in astonishment. His stomach lurched. One last look at the bloody mess of a man lying there right in front of him was enough. He rushed out into the hallway and started throwing up. Each time he closed his eyes in pain, he could see Jerry O'Neill there, shot to death. A bloody pulp.

"I gotta go."

Hamlin was terrified he might be next. His only response was to try and get out of that house of death as quickly as possible. But Paul Jenkins had other ideas.

"You're not goin' nowhere. You gotta help me move him."

The very thought of going back into that bedroom filled him with fear. The idea of seeing Jerry O'Neill lying there was an awful prospect. But Paul Jenkins was insistent. He grabbed his workmate by the arm and dragged him back into the bedroom. Together they wrapped the corpse in the very quilts that Jerry O'Neill used to collapse on when he was too drunk to even get undressed. Then, using rope to tie up each end, they carried the body out to Jerry O'Neill's own van. Neither of them noticed the trail of blood that marked their route from the bedroom out into the yard.

"Where the hell are we goin' to take him?"

It was a perfectly reasonable question, considering the circumstances. Bereaved widow Maxine just did not know the answer to Paul Jenkins's question. She had not even thought about that aspect of their crime. She had just wanted her husband dead. Who cared about where to dump his body?

But it was a crucial point. Paul Jenkins knew that the only way they stood a chance of getting away with the murder was if they found the perfect hiding place for the corpse. Then he remembered some of the creeks and canyons in Stone County, where he had been brought up as a boy. Some of those areas were so isolated that no-one would ever find it.

"I know some good places. Let's go."

So, together, the hired hand and his mistress set off on a wild trek upstate hundreds of miles to find the perfect spot to dump her dead husband.

They hardly spoke during the night. She kept reassuring herself that Jerry O'Neill had deserved to die. She remembered all the sexual perversion, the drunkenness, the assaults. She had to keep convincing herself she had done the right thing. As she snuggled up alongside Paul Jenkins while he drove through the driving rain, she felt relieved. At last her hellish marriage was over. She could start a new life with Paul. It had to be better than the one she had just left behind.

"This is perfect. Let's stop and take a look."

Maxine O'Neill was jolted from her reassuring fantasies by Jenkins's assertion that they might have finally found the perfect resting place for Jerry O'Neill.

At night the area looked awesome. A huge cliff dipping down into a valley that probably could have accommodated the whole of South-East England. As Paul Jenkins looked out over the cliff edge, he felt the cold breeze blowing against his face. He turned to Maxine and held her in his arms as they considered how best to hide the body.

132

They just stood there listening to the whistling wind for a while. Reality had taken a back seat at that moment. They were in the middle of nowhere — literally. Maxine felt more secure than she would have thought possible a few months previously.

After a while, they both snapped out of their romantic trance and decided to get on with the job in hand. By the time they pulled the duvet-covered body out of the van, blood had seeped right through in huge dark stains and the smell was very pungent. It was a sickly, sweet aroma — like a joint of meat that's been left out in the sun for a day.

They turned away and walked back to the van the moment after they had dropped the body off the edge of the cliff. If they had waited to watch its descent, they would have seen that it only fell about fifty feet before getting caught on a ledge that looked out onto the valley below.

On the drive back home, Maxine even announced that she thought her husband was very lucky to have found his final resting place in such a picturesque spot.

"I would have been more than happy to end my days there. It was beautiful."

Paul Jenkins listened intently to his new love. It seemed a very strange thing to say.

Back at the house next morning, they quickly cleaned up the mess left behind by the bloody remains of Jerry O'Neill. Maxine even managed to remove the blood stains from the carpet.

Finally, there was one last crucial piece of evidence that had to be disposed of — the mattress on which Maxine's husband had bled to death after being shot.

It was far too big to hide, so the couple struggled through the house with it and laid it on a bonfire in the back garden and watched it burn. Maxine realised it was the last thing around that linked them to the death of her husband.

Just to round things off, she ordered a new mattress

133

to be delivered that very same day. By seven o'clock that evening Maxine O'Neill and Paul Jenkins had already sealed their love for one another on the same bed where Jerry O'Neill had been shot just twenty-four hours earlier.

Within days, Maxine announced to her friends and relatives, with genuine relief, that she had given her husband $20,000 to "drop off the face of the earth". She told all who asked, that Jerry O'Neill was in Louisiana.

And when Sheriff David Baker of Pike County Police came knocking on her door to investigate rumours that were wildly circulating about the real fate of Jerry O'Neill, she could not have been more charming.

"I'll get Jerry to call you when I next hear from him."

Sheriff Baker was not that surprised when the call from O'Neill never materialised. But he could not arrest Maxine or her farm-hand lover without evidence of a crime — and there was still no sign of Jerry O'Neill.

For five months, the finger of suspicion was frequently pointed at Maxine and both Jenkins and Hamlin. But no-one could do a damn thing about it. Even when Maxine sold the farm, the bar and all the cattle for close to $250,000, there was nothing anyone could do.

But then not many people realised that Maxine only ended up with around $50,000 in her pocket, because of the massive debts incurred by Jerry O'Neill and his businesses.

Then, two children out walking near that cliff in Stone County made a gruesome discovery — the partly decomposed body of Jerry O'Neill, still wrapped in those two duvets that came from the farmhouse. Now, at last, Sheriff Baker had the evidence he needed. The only problem was that his two main suspects had long since disappeared.

For five months, Maxine O'Neill and Paul Jenkins

eluded a massive police hunt for them. She dyed her hair peroxide blonde, lost weight and took on an entirely new identity. He grew his hair longer and added a beard to the moustache. They rapidly managed to make themselves look completely different from just a few months earlier. It proved very effective in helping them avoid arrest.

But then the inevitable happened — they started to run short of funds. The $50,000 just did not stretch far enough. Maxine was reduced to trying to persuade a relative to wire them some cash to the tiny town of Pelham, Alabama.

When the two wanted killers showed up to collect their money, they were immediately picked up by local police.

In September, 1990, at the Pike County Courthouse, Maxine O'Neill·admitted to the killing of her husband and was given a ten-year sentence with three years suspended and a $10,000 fine.

Paul Jenkins was found guilty of first-degree murder and sentenced to twenty years in jail.

During her trial, Maxine told the jury she loved Jenkins and planned to marry him as soon as prison authorities allowed the ceremony to go ahead.

9
Naked Fear

Santa Barbara, California, is one of those beachside paradises most people can only dream about. Miles and miles of pure white sand overlooking the Pacific Ocean. A picturesque seafront town with a scattering of bars and restaurants attractively designed to guarantee hundreds of thousands of visitors each summer. Immaculately clean pavements and streets kept pristine by a city council that insists on nothing but the best. And famous in Britain as the setting for possibly the worst soap opera ever written.

Yet Santa Barbara is situated just two hours' drive north of the sprawling metropolis of Los Angeles and all its well publicised problems. That means the local police are always on the lookout for troublemakers entering their little piece of heaven-by-the-sea. Santa Barbara is primarily known as a family-orientated town but beneath that wholesome exterior lies a seedy underbelly typical of any seaside community from Brighton to Benidorm.

And, according to many locals, the "distasteful" elements included the notorious El Capitan beach just outside town. For this was where the home values and strait-laced beliefs of so much of Middle America were thrown out of the window. In a country where bare breasts are censored on prime-time television yet mass killings are considered fair game, the El Capitan beach was a place that people only referred to in hushed tones. You see, it was a good, old-fashioned nudist beach.

Lots of nature lovers would saunter down to the isolated beauty spot and strip off in a desperate bid for that famous all-over tan. Interestingly, the majority of visitors to El Capitan were middle-aged. Youngsters seemed to avoid the place like the plague. It must have been their puritanical upbringing that did it.

Remember, more than seventy per cent of America's population still go to church every Sunday!

Phillip Bogdanoff and his pretty wife Diana were two such avid sun worshippers. They loved making the short trip from their mobile home at El Capitan Beach Ranch Park, which overlooked the sea. In fact, it was a dream come true for Phillip. He had a healthy — some people would say unhealthy — interest in examining the figures of all those nude beachgoers. He was always subtly casting his gaze across the perfectly formed muscles and firm thighs of some of the beach's other, more fanatical, visitors.

The handsome, rugged, fun-loving 49-year-old engineer kept himself in pretty good shape, too. He was extremely proud of his body and relished the chance to strip off completely. He had been a regular at the beach for many years when he met attractive fair-haired Diana in nearby Colefax, California. She was working as a nursing aide at a nearby convalescent hospital when they met in 1984. A four-year courtship followed, during which they learned just about everything there was to know about each other. Both had suffered broken marriages, so they were understandably cautious at first. In any case, Diana already had children from her previous husband, so there was no hurry to tie the knot.

Eventually, in February, 1989, they married and moved to their dream location right opposite the most infamous beach in Santa Barbara. And whenever they were not working during that summer, Diana and Phillip loved to pack a towel and set off on the short walk down to El Capitan.

Phillip had been so relieved when Diana voiced absolutely no objections to stripping off in a public place. He even had a sneaking suspicion that she rather enjoyed exhibiting her body to the beach population that tended to consist of rather more men than women. Sometimes Phillip would catch healthily endowed guys staring at his wife's pert body and smile at them, before they could avert their gaze in embarrassment at being "caught" peeping.

Diana, for her part, would sometimes sneakily open her legs just a fraction if she knew some of the more handsome specimens were watching at her eye-level. She got a thrill out of letting them see just a hint. Phillip seemed to know precisely what his wife was playing at and he gave it his own bizarre seal of approval by just observing — and enjoying — the proceedings.

Their other favourite pastime was frolicking in the warm ocean. They both agreed that nude swimming was a hell of a refreshing way to pass the time. Diana and Phillip loved that feeling when the water rushed past them, sending surf crashing all over their skin. They used to say it was second only to making love.

But, back on the beach during those swelteringly hot summer months of 1989, Diana often used to let her mind wander to other, less innocent, things as she sunbathed. She would close her eyes in the bright sunlight and think about...those passionate sex sessions with the manager of the trailer park.

She ran her tongue down his neck and over his right nipple before biting gently into his soft skin. Then she moved back to his mouth and started probing deeply with her tongue. Running the tip right across his gums, flicking it rapidly back and forth.

Then she opened her own mouth as wide as possible so that he could plunge his tongue halfway down her throat. The passion between them was endless. Diana Bogdanoff did not once consider her new husband, lying on the nudist beach just a few hundred yards away.

She had only met the man a few days earlier when he helped them move into their new home. But he caught her looking him up and down and knew

138

they would end up in bed together.

Now, Diana was enjoying what she liked doing best — making hot, steamy love with a rampant male. Naturally, she was on top most of the time. She loved to tease and tantalise them. Make them come really close to climaxing then let go for a split second. It always made them beg for more.

The irony was that her husband of just a few months was on that nearby nudist beach ogling at naked bodies, probably in a highly excitable state. But she preferred to relax another man's tension.

Back in the trailer that day, she was giving the park manager the sort of servicing he had previously only dreamed about. She was willing and prepared to do anything to please him, just so long as she stayed in charge. As they lay there, hot and sweaty after hours of love-making, she sat up and looked through the window at that notorious beach across the street and smiled to herself. Her husband got his pleasure watching naked bodies. She got her enjoyment from performing the real thing. It made her realise that her marriage was a sham — something she should never have gotten herself into. She started thinking of a way out of it.

"If you wanted to kill someone, how would you do it?"

Her secret lover thought he was hearing things. Did she really just suggest she wanted to kill someone, moments after enjoying sex?

"Come on. A guy like you must know how it can be done."

Still he did not reply. The sex between them may well have been out of this world but when she started talking about murdering her husband he began to wonder what sort of relationship he had got himself involved in.

Diana was not deterred by his reluctance to reply. Her mind was set on that particular subject. There was no two ways about it. She was trying to devise a way to kill her husband.

"I thought about lacing his food with cocaine. D'you think that might work?"

"I doubt it. He'd probably just end up getting high and havin' a great time."

"What about poison? What d'you reckon would be the best brand to use?"

Her illicit lover could hardly believe his ears. Here he was, enjoying a highly charged, sexual affair with an attractive 40-year-old woman and all she wanted to talk about was how to murder her husband!

So he played along with her "game". She could not possibly be serious.

"You wanna try getting some of that poison from those pencil trees that grow out near Morro Bay."

He could not believe he had just said that. Now he was starting to encourage her to do it. He stopped in his tracks. Enough was enough.

"Hey, that's a great idea. Will you come with me and help me find some of those trees?"

Her secret mobile-home lover shook his head vehemently.

"No way. You must be crazy. Forget it. Get a divorce if you're so unhappy."

Diana got out of bed in a sulky silence, put her clothes on and headed out of the one and only door to that trailer. She was furious that he would not help her. She would have to find someone else to help hatch her callous plan.

"He's beaten me and abused me more than I can handle. I gotta do something."

Diana Bogdanoff was pretty convincing as a battered wife, especially when the person she was appealing to was her stunningly attractive 18-year-old daughter Stephanie. The gorgeous dark-haired teenager sat rivetted by her mother's appalling revelations. How could her step-father be such a beast?

"You gotta help me kill him. It's the only way."

"But, mom. That's murder you're talkin' about. Just

get away from him. Just leave him."

"But I've got nothing. If I leave him I'll be out on the streets. If we kill him, at least I'll get to keep the house and all our money and things."

"You're crazy!"

Like any self-respecting daughter, Stephanie was genuinely worried about her mother's safety at the hands of her allegedly brutal husband. She feared for her safety, but to murder him did seem rather drastic. However, Diana Bogdanoff could sense her daughter's misplaced sympathy beginning to grow. She gave up her first attempt to organise the killing but there would be other opportunities.

At least three more times, Diana called up her daughter at her home fifty miles away in Bakersfield and begged her to help her end her husband's life.

On the first two occasions she got the same reply — a definite "No way". But on the third attempt, Stephanie took heed of the real panic in her mother's voice and she gave in.

"I know this isn't right but if it's the only way then I guess we'll have to do it."

Diana Bogdanoff was so happy. The longer she spent with Phillip, the more she realised how much she despised him. The only time when she did not feel such a deep hatred for him was when they lay on that nudist beach surrounded by bare bodies, and she would close her eyes and part her legs ever so slightly and start to think back to her passionate interludes with other men.

Stephanie was in overall charge of their mission and she chose her long-time admirer Raymond Stock to carry out the execution. He was so besotted with the shapely, long-legged teenager that he was prepared to sacrifice his liberty for her.

"There isn't anything I wouldn't do for you," Stock told Stephanie when she put her mother's extraordinary request to him.

141

But his love obsession for her was somewhat sweetened by the promise of $10,000 and part-ownership of a house.

As the stunning looking Stephanie snuggled up close to Stock on the settee at his home, she playfully stroked his thigh and said: "I promise we'll be together afterwards and I'll give you the time of your life."

The scene was set. Now the besotted lover had to go out and prove he really was the man of her dreams.

Within hours they had stolen a car, switched its number plates and pointed the bumper in the direction of Santa Barbara. As they drove the one-hour trip, they talked in vivid detail about the plan to murder Phillip Bogdanoff.

It was pretty simple really. Go to his mobile home, wait for him to open the door and pump him full of bullets. But Stock started to get an uneasy feeling as Stephanie clinically talked her way through every move. He had a sick kind of feeling in his stomach. As they approached the outskirts of Santa Barbara, his conscience got the better of him. The idea of blasting Phillip Bogdanoff to death seemed all wrong. His hands were shaking. Even with Stephanie snuggled close to him as they drove. Kissing and licking his ears, neck and cheeks throughout the journey. There was no way he could do it. The same thought kept going through Stock's mind: "I'll go to hell if I do this."

When he told Stephanie he was pulling out of it, she was surprisingly calm. They turned the car around and headed back to Bakersfield in total silence. When he dropped her off at her home, she had already decided that she would never see Stock again. He had just paid the ultimate price for not carrying out what he had promised.

Within a few days, though, Stephanie had enticed another of the men so besotted with her. This time his name was Danny Kaplan, another neighbour from Bakersfield. He said later that there was something

142

incredibly alluring about the teenager. When she nuzzled up to him and said she needed a favour, he couldn't wait to help. Even after she had explained the task at hand, he took a big gulp and decided to carry out the dirty deed, all in the name of love.

"I loved her so much I'd have done anything for her," said Kaplan later. It was a familiar story. Stephanie had that sort of effect on men.

He did not even object when Stephanie said her regular boyfriend, 21-year-old Brian Stafford, would be accompanying them on their quest for murder. Kaplan's love for her was so strong he would have put up with anything. He really believed he would be her only true love in the end.

A few days after that, they both loaded shotguns and rifles into Kaplan's car and headed back towards Santa Barbara. This time the plan was to blast Phillip Bogdanoff to death as he drove alongside them on the motorway on his way back home from work.

By the time they arrived near the office where he worked, all three were pretty hyped up about what was about to happen. They sat in a discreet vantage point overlooking the main entrance to the building and waited for Bogdanoff to come out.

Hours passed by and still there was no sign of him leaving the office. Soon, darkness fell and the three accomplices began to realise that maybe he was not even there. They started to get agitated. And Kaplan began to wonder what on earth he was doing there in the first place.

"Let's call it a day. We'll have to think up a different way to do this."

Stephanie, as usual, was very much in charge. As the two men bundled their mini-armoury of weapons back into the boot of the car, she began trying to work out a different way of killing her "evil" stepfather. But all those hours of waiting had a different kind of effect on Kaplan.

"I'm not going through with it. I can't do it."

143

Stephanie and her boyfriend Brian Stafford were astonished by Kaplan's outburst. Here they all were about to assassinate a man and one member of the hit team was getting cold feet.

"Come on. You promised. We all agreed."

Stephanie made it sound more like a playground dare than a mission to murder.

"No way. I cannot murder an innocent man."

"But he's not innocent. He's beaten my mom. He deserves to die."

"You don't know that for sure."

Stephanie tried in vain to persuade Kaplan to the contrary, but it was no good. They had lost a crucial team player. They would have to go back to the drawing board yet again.

But nothing would stop Stephanie from going ahead with it in the end. She just would not give up. All the ominous signs were clearly there. But she ignored them all out of a fierce loyalty for her "battered" mother. The right opportunity would come along eventually.

And boyfriend Stafford was still as passionate about Stephanie as ever. He would do anything for her, in exchange for the romance he so desperately wanted to keep going.

Just a few weeks later on September 21, 1989, Stephanie, Stafford and his great pal Ricky Rogers teamed up for what they hoped would be a third-time lucky bid to murder Phillip Bogdanoff.

On this occasion, the plan had changed somewhat. The two men were going to head for the Bogdanoffs' favourite beach at El Capitan.

That day had started off perfectly normally for Diana and Phillip Bogdanoff. The hot September sun had, not surprisingly, enticed the couple out onto the beach, where they could not resist stripping off all their clothes and trying to top up their all-over tans.

144

El Capitan was pretty busy that day. The surf was crashing down, forming huge slicks of bubbly froth on the sand as dozens of sunworshippers lay completely naked on their specially reserved strip of beach.

Diana and Phillip took up their favourite spot just a few yards from the water's edge. It was the perfect location for him to cast his eyes across the beautiful oiled bodies soaking up the sunshine. Diana was a little more tetchy than usual. She found it difficult to lie still. But then there was rather a lot on her mind that day.

Instead of laying flat on her back as she normally did, Diana found herself sitting up with her knees close to her breasts as she watched the crowds from a distance. Watching. Waiting. Watching. Waiting.

When Phillip looked up, he noticed his wife's behaviour but simply took it as further evidence that she was coming around to his way of thinking. Bodies were beautiful to look at. It never once crossed his mind that she was actually looking out for two particularly over-covered bodies.

The trouble was the more she looked out for her accomplices, the more she found herself ogling the naked men stretched out in the immediate vicinity. She got quite embarrassed when one guy started trying to give her the come on because she had been gazing past his right shoulder at two men loitering near the beach wall.

She only looked away when they came close enough for her to see that they were the very people she had been waiting for. Reassured that her command was finally about to be carried out, she lay on her back and relaxed. A warm smile was all she was wearing as she lay there and started to fantasise about life without him. It was 11am and there were only a few minutes left of Phillip Bogdanoff's life.

"Hey, man. You gotta joint?"

The two men were standing right over the naked

145

figures of Diana and Phillip Bogdanoff, blocking the sun from carrying out its duty to give them that essential all-over tan.

"I'm sorry. What did you say?"

Phillip was not even sure he had heard them right.

"I said: You got some grass?"

Phillip was more a martini type of character. Cannabis had never been on his social menu.

"I don't smoke."

He was nervous of these two men. There was something about them. They seemed to be preparing to do something, but Phillip Bogdanoff did not know what. Diana did not move. She lay there saying nothing.

Just then, the two men looked at each other nervously. The quiet one pulled a pistol and pointed it straight at Bogdanoff in silence and pulled the trigger.

The bullet ripped through his cheek, spinning him off balance. That first wound was neat but ineffective. Brian Stafford moved even nearer to his victim and fired again. This time Phillip Bogdanoff's head recoiled and he slumped to the ground.

"All I wanted to do was stop his pain," said Brian Stafford later when trying to justify why he fired that second shot.

Back on the beach that day, Diana Bogdanoff screamed in terror. She might have set the whole thing up but the reality of the murder was still enough to spark off her emotions. The most horrifying evidence of the killing was her husband's blood splattered all over her naked breasts and stomach. She looked down at herself and shrieked.

Gunman Stafford coolly and calmly put his pistol back inside his shirt and started to disappear down the beach with his accomplice. Their mission had been completed. They heard her cries for help and looked around for a moment and saw her kneeling, naked and bloody, over the corpse of her husband — the man she had ordered them to kill.

Within minutes the secluded calm of that naturists' paradise had been cruelly destroyed by hundreds of police, paramedics, coroners' officers, press and onlookers desperately trying to get a glimpse of the grisly sight of a naked guy blasted to bits on the beach in front of his wife.

Just a few yards from where her husband had been killed, sat the shaking figure of Diana Bogdanoff. Wearing a pullover to cover her blood-splattered skin, the hysterical widow was being comforted by a tourist who just happened to be walking by moments after the shooting and had immediately offered her his jumper for cover.

"They shot my husband. They shot my husband."

She just kept repeating the words over and over again. It was an impressive performance. The truth is that she probably did feel bereaved and shocked in a weird way, because talking about murder is a whole lot different than going through with it.

Through rivers of tears, Diana told police of the two complete strangers who came up to her husband and ended his life just because he told them he did not smoke pot.

"Phillip didn't do anything," she weeped. "He didn't say anything to make them angry. He was just sitting there."

Detectives were baffled and they all said how sorry they felt for that poor, grieving widow.

"It seemed a senseless cruel killing," said one cop on the TV news that night. The town of Santa Barbara was under a state of siege by the media, and some residents genuinely feared that the mystery killers might strike again at any time and any place.

But the only place Brian Stafford and his friend Ricky Rogers were heading was back to their homes in Bakersfield, with the beautiful Stephanie alongside them in the car.

As far as she was concerned, this was a time to

celebrate. She had helped her poor, battered mother get out of a nightmare marriage to a monster. And Diana would still have a home to live in and a good income from his life insurance.

When the murdering threesome arrived back at Stephanie's home she broke open a few beers and proposed a toast.

"To a job well done."

The beer bottles clinked in unison. Their mission had been accomplished.

Then they switched on the television and found exactly what they were looking for. A suitably distressed Diana Bogdanoff pouring out her heart and soul to the TV news cameras as she played an Oscar-winning role as the tragic widow. She shed more tears, wrung her hands and gave a wonderfully convincing performance.

The three killers looked on and laughed. It had all gone so smoothly they could hardly believe it had really happened.

Within a few minutes Ricky Rogers had left, and Stephanie climbed into bed with her athletic lover and switched her attention to a pastime her mother would definitely have approved of.

Detectives Russ Birchim and Fred Ray were seasoned homicide cops who had investigated just about every type of murder over the years. But the slaying in cold blood of Phillip Bogdanoff truly baffled them.

As one of them said: "No-one gets killed over a joint. Certainly not in a nudist beach in broad daylight."

There was only one conclusion as far as they were concerned: Bogdanoff's wife had something to do with it.

But Diana was not about to throw away her entire life by confessing to a crime she knew they could not pin on her. She stuck rigidly to her story about the "tragic" death of her loving husband.

Neighbours at the El Capitan Ranch Park had only

good things to say about the Bogdanoffs. "Nice couple." "Kept themselves to themselves." "A sweet pair." They could do no wrong in the eyes of those who knew them.

Detectives Birchim and Ray plugged away with composite sketches of the two killers based on eye-witnesses' reports. Hundreds of likely looking suspects were pulled in, interrogated and cleared. The investigation went on like that for a month.

Birchim and Ray chewed over a few other possible theories. Maybe the two gunmen were a couple of screwballs who were high on dope? Perhaps it was all a case of mistaken identity?

But, whatever their suspicions about the case, there was no hard and fast evidence to go on. The two cops were swimming around in the dark.

Then an anonymous caller phoned in to a police informants' hotline in Bakersfield. The man said he had information about the nude beach murder in Santa Barbara.

"I thought they were joking," he told the police operator. "Then I saw the newspaper reports and realised they had done it."

The tipster then told the operator the names of the people he claimed were involved. The first one on his list was Raymond Stock, the man who had been involved in the initial abortive attempt on the life of Phillip Bogdanoff.

When detectives called at his home in Bakersfield he confessed that he had almost killed Bogdanoff.

The next one on the list was Danny Kaplan. He had a similar story to tell. But this time he furnished the police with the names of Stafford and his pal Ricky Rogers, as well as ringleader Stephanie.

Kaplan even told officers how Stafford, Rogers and Stephanie came back to her apartment after the actual killing, bragging about what they had just done.

"They were saying: 'We did it. We did it. We blew the sucker away'."

149

Kaplan had sat there listening to them with a sinking feeling in his stomach. He knew full well who they were talking about.

Within days, the gang of assassins had been rounded up and by the time Diana Bogdanoff returned from a trip to visit relatives in Washington state, the police were there at the airport to greet her.

For months she stuck rigidly to her story that she was innocent of any involvement in her husband's death. Then her first husband came forward and revealed that when the couple had divorced in 1980, she had told him:

"You're lucky you're still alive. I tried to hire two men to kill you."

For Diana Bogdanoff, killing lovers and husbands had been an obsession for years. It just took the perfect opportunity for her to realise her lifetime ambition.

In March, 1991, at the Santa Barbara County Superior Court, Stephanie pleaded guilty to second-degree murder and received a fifteen-year-to-life sentence. Boyfriend Brian Stafford pleaded guilty to first-degree murder and got thirty-three years after agreeing to testify against Diana Bogdanoff. In June, 1991, Ricky Rogers entered a plea of no contest to one charge of voluntary manslaughter. He was sentenced to no more than ten years in jail because he did not pull the trigger.

Meanwhile, in October, 1990, Diana Bogdanoff went on trial at the same courthouse. After hours of deliberation, the judge pronounced a mistrial because the jury could not agree on a verdict. At her second trial in May, 1991, jurors took just two hours to find her guilty of first-degree murder. She was also found guilty of planning the murder for financial gain and lying in wait for the killing to take place. Under those "special circumstances", she was given an automatic life sentence without parole.

10

"Ma Baker"

Male nurse Leonard Rose hated working the night shift at the Clarke Institute of Psychiatry, in Toronto, Canada. It was not an easy place at the best of times, but there was something about the night-time that brought out the worst in some of the more difficult patients. His rounds at the hospital included the carefully segregated male and female wards. Each hour, he would quietly patrol the immaculately clean corridors that were separated by a pair of swing doors. It was a tedious task in many ways but it had to be done, otherwise all sorts of dangerous scenarios could occur.

The Clarke — as it was known locally — was filled with a bizarre mish-mash of inmates ranging from convicted criminals judged to be bordering on insanity, to voluntary patients trying to prevent themselves from sliding into serious psychiatric problems. The stresses and strains of living in the modern world had proved too much for many of these individuals. Some were, inevitably, victims — abused as children, driven to commit crimes because of their own lack of self-esteem, sexual perverts with no other place to turn.

On a hot summer's night in August, 1986, Nurse Leonard Rose was more concerned with maintaining a quiet life, if you can call working in a psychiatric hospital that. As the sun rose and early morning rays peeped through the wafer-thin hospital curtains, Leonard began his sixth and final tour of the wards before finishing his shift. He was really looking forward to getting home to a hearty breakfast and a few hours' sleep.

As was his usual procedure, Leonard began his round by checking through the forensic unit of the hospital. By the time he got to the main men's ward, it was around 7am. All was quiet — if anything, too

151

quiet. He cast his eyes along the row of beds on each side of the ward to make sure everyone was accounted for. Suddenly, Nurse Rose did a double take. One of the inmates was absent from his bed. He walked briskly towards the empty bed, just to make sure he was right. But there was absolutely no sign of Bruce Lynch — a convicted armed robber, who was considered a "high-security" inmate even by Clarke standards.

Nurse Rose rushed to the men's room and methodically checked each cubicle to see if Lynch was there but somehow he knew, even before he entered the bathroom, that the inmate would be nowhere in sight. Leonard remembered that another nurse had told him about problems they had encountered involving an illicit romance between Lynch and a female inmate called Harriet Giesecke.

He dashed over to the female ward, convinced that they were up to something. He cast his eyes along the row of beds in room 401 to see if Giesecke was there. She was nowhere to be spotted. He walked towards her bed, looking for clues.

Harriet Giesecke and Bruce Lynch could hardly contain their giggles as they lay naked beneath that very same bed. Nurse Leonard was carrying out a frantic search for them but they did not give a damn. Instead, Harriet opened her legs even wider so that Lynch could penetrate deeper into her.

She bit into his shoulder to stop Nurse Rose from hearing her moans of pleasure. Her hands slapped and pinched his bottom before pulling him even deeper into her. She could feel his tongue exploring the cavities of her ear. Neither of them cared that just a few feet away were dozens of female inmates and Nurse Rose. Maybe it was out and out exhibitionism. Or perhaps they were simply so desperate to seal their love for one another that they had to do it anywhere, any place.

Whatever the reason, no-one was about to stop 30-year-old Harriet Giesecke from getting exactly what she wanted. As she lay there, legs spread wide apart under that rusting metal hospital bed, her thoughts were consumed by one, over riding emotion — passion. As she got closer and closer to a climax, so the fear of being caught subsided to the point where she did not care.

Harriet bit deep into Lynch's shoulder at the moment of ultimate satisfaction. She could not stop herself thrusting her hips up towards him in an effort to squeeze every drop of excitement out of their embrace.

She was virtually oblivious to the world when Nurse Leonard Rose stooped down and peered under the bed, having at last found his two missing inmates.

"Stop it now!" Rose yelled so loud that many of the patients woke with a start. The ones who had already been fully conscious just sniggered as they watched Harriet's white quivering knees still spread apart by a man's bottom thrusting up and down.

Bruce Lynch, aged 25, hesitantly withdrew from Harriet and climbed out from under the bed, looking a bit sheepish to say the least. As he stood up next to Nurse Rose and wrapped a hospital dressing-gown around himself, he looked down at Harriet, still lying spread-eagled on the cold vinyl floor, and smiled. It was a smile that could best be described as being very similar to that of a cat that just drank it's last drop of cream from a plate.

"Come on. Get up now!"

Nurse Rose was in no mood to be sensitive to Harriet's embarrassing position. But then Harriet did not seem that bothered either. She ever so casually got up from the floor and brushed past the male nurse, much to the amusement of virtually every other inmate in room 401 that morning.

But Bruce Lynch was not the only man in the Clarke Institute who was madly in love with Harriet Giesecke.

Her brown, wavy hair and neat facial features certainly distinguished her from most of the worn, thin, haggard female faces in that daunting hospital. She had quickly caught the eye of Ron Nicholl, another seasoned criminal bordering on the insane. He and Lynch became known as Harriet's "boys" and, perhaps not so surprisingly, she soon got nicknamed "Ma Baker".

Harriet had voluntarily checked herself in to the Clarke Institute to try and sort out various "psychiatric problems" that had troubled her for many years and led her into a lot of minor trouble with the law.

But the truth was that she probably rather enjoyed life inside the Clarke's four walls because it was a world where responsibilities were kept to a minimum. You didn't need money, there were no bills, there was little emotion. It was simple, really; you did pretty well what you liked, within the confines of a hospital filled to the brim with seriously disturbed people. To Harriet even that bizarre world was preferable to life on the outside — she had left her husband Randy and their baby daughter Erica many months previously and just ended up drifting from job to job and bed to bed. Now, in the Clarke, none of those problems were weighing her down. Her biggest dilemma was when to check out of the hospital and face the outside world once more.

She had gradually built up a loathing and hatred towards her husband for kicking her out and taking her pretty little daughter away from her. Doctors said it was these problems that drove Harriet into the arms of renegades like Lynch and Nicholl. Relatives and friends said it was purely down to her insatiable appetite for sex. Whatever the truth, Harriet Giesecke had a fairly outrageous reputation at the Clarke, especially after that sex incident under the bed with Lynch.

Harriet loved the attention all the men were constantly giving her. She adored to feel them lusting after her as she swaggered her shapely hips along the corridors of the Clarke. She knew that patients and staff alike were all well aware of her sexual promiscuity and that made her feel good. She had spent her entire life longing for love and attention. In that grim, grey place she was getting huge doses of that.

But Harriet also had another motive for flirting with Nicholl and Lynch. In her role as "Ma Baker", she wanted to persuade them to commit a crime so horrendous that it would affect them all for the rest of their living days.

"I'll give you $5,000 — cash."

Lynch and Nicholl listened open-mouthed as the woman they both lusted after so much made them an astonishing offer to murder her husband Randy.

Harriet Giesecke wanted the two hard men to kill her husband because she was determined to stop him having sole custody of their child.

"He beat me so bad that I had to leave the house, but he's still got my daughter and God knows what he's doin' to her."

It was a fairly convincing story. But, all the same, Harriet was trying to hire two men to commit the ultimate crime. It was not a decision that any person could take lightly.

"Why don't you just take off with the baby? Seems much easier than murder to me."

Ron Nicholl seemed to be making much more sense than Harriet. But the attractive brunette just could not see it that way.

"The cops'll come after me. I'll never get far. No. Killin' him's much easier."

Nicholl did not reply. He watched as his love rival Bruce Lynch nodded his head hesitantly. At that moment Ron Nicholl decided it was time to split from "Ma Baker" and her "boys." Murder was not something he wanted to get involved in.

Harriet Giesecke was disappointed but not put off by Nicholl's refusal to get involved. She resolved there and then to check out of the Clarke Institute and wait for her lover Lynch to get out, so they could commit the perfect crime together.

Randy Giesecke had been heartbroken when his marriage to Harriet crumbled. They had met a few years earlier when he was married to another woman and he'd given up his family and a safe, comfortable, suburban life to be with the intelligent Harriet. She had swept him off his feet with her sensuous advances. She had told him about her rich parents and the luxury lifestyle she had enjoyed as a kid growing up in Michigan. It all seemed like a fairy-tale romance during those first few happy months, but the cracks soon began to appear in their relationship.

To begin with, Randy — a 31-year-old life insurance salesman — discovered that his new wife's claims of great wealth were no more than a huge sham. The truth was far more hard for him to swallow — she was a convicted petty criminal with a long record of problems with the police.

Then she got pregnant and Randy hoped that this might help Harriet to settle down to a normal life. He genuinely wanted their marriage to work and was delighted when she announced she was pregnant. Maybe a child might help seal their rocky relationship.

But the truth was that the birth of beautiful little Erica in April, 1985, provided no more than a brief respite from Harriet's outrageous activities. Within a few weeks of her birth, the couple were arguing virtually every minute of the day. Most of the rows were about money. The problem was that Harriet had set herself up in such a bizarre fantasy world of the rich and famous that she could not handle the reality of the situation, which was that they were a financially stretched young family. Just like everyone else. But Harriet could not accept that. She didn't want to be normal. It was dull. -It lacked edge.

It was no real surprise to Randy or his parents

when Harriet stormed out of their modest home in Scarborough, just north-east of Toronto. And the bitter custody battle for little Erica that followed was something that, sadly, millions of couples throughout the world seem to experience after the break up of a marriage. But that did not make it any less painful for either of the heartbroken parents. Randy, the responsible one with the safe job and the steady reputation, against Harriet, the fantasy merchant with a criminal record as long as her arm — it was hardly surprising when the courts looked set to award Randy full custody of the child. But, tragically, Harriet's fear of that decision probably contributed most of all to his eventual brutal departure from this earth.

The custody split sparked a feeling of overwhelming bitterness inside Harriet's mind. She felt betrayed by the system, even though in reality she never stood the remotest chance of gaining the right to bring up her own daughter. She convinced herself that it was all a conspiracy against her. She felt trapped in a world where she had nothing to offer. The pride had dropped out of her life. As the bitterness mounted, so her animal cunning began to take over the logical parts of her mind.

Even after she moved in with her husband's aunt, who was supposed to be a calming influence, the anger and resentment just continued to build within her.

One day, when her husband came by his aunt's to pick up Erica after a rare visit to her mother, Harriet followed him home to ensure she had an address for her estranged husband. She had been barred by the court from being allowed to know his address because there were genuine fears she might snatch the child. But that was not her intention in following Randy home. She was laying the seeds for a death trap. But her plans had only just begun...

Randy Giesecke was never one to ignore an opportunity to earn a little extra commission in his job as a life insurance salesman. So when a man called Mike Simmons rang him up and asked him if he'd come round to give him and his wife Susan a quote later that day, Randy was only too delighted to oblige.

The address Mr Simmons gave was 164 Hollyberry Trail. If only Randy had realised that it did not exist. But then Harriet Giesecke simply wanted to lure her estranged husband to the street where her lover lived and then blast him to bits for ever.

"I should be back in about an hour."

Randy Giesecke was leaving instructions for the baby-sitter at the immaculate flat he lived in with baby daughter Erica, when the phone rang. It was "Mr Simmons" again, cancelling their arrangement. Randy was disappointed. He had been hoping to sign up the Simmonses for a really hefty life insurance policy, and that would have helped pay for some special new clothes for his beloved Erica. He had no idea that the second "Mr Simmons" call was also a phoney — investigated by Harriet after she realised that she could not cold-bloodedly kill her husband in the street. She would have to think of some other way of trapping him in a dark and isolated spot...

Harriet Giesecke knew precisely where her husband parked his Ford pick-up truck in the underground car park to the apartment block where he lived. She quietly pulled her own car to a halt in the space next to his and switched off the engine and waited. It was September 22, 1986, just a few days away from that final custody hearing that would confirm all her worst fears. Harriet Giesecke sat there patiently, in no particular hurry. She could wait. He would come home from work eventually, and then she would get him.

She felt the excitement working through her system. She clutched the sawn-off shotgun between her legs, switched on the radio cassette and pressed fast forward until she found her favourite song. She did not care how long it would take. She was not even worried that the silver Honda Accord she was driving had been stolen by her lover Lynch from an exgirlfriend of his. The cops were hardly likely to patrol an underground car park.

It was 6.30pm. Harriet nuzzled the warm wooden handle of that shotgun against herself and pressed her legs together tightly, in anticipation of what was about to happen. It was a strange sensation — a blend of fear and excitement that was working its way through her. She rocked back and forth in time to the heavy metal music on the cassette and shut her eyes for a few moments. She could see the happy, smiling face of her daughter now. She could see them all together in happier days. She wished she could turn the clock back but it was too late.

Harriet's trance was broken by the screech of a tyre on the dry surface of that car park. It was followed by the deep revving noise of a powerful V8 engine. Then the tyres screeched again as the car headed up the ramp towards where she was parked. Her eyes squinted against the glare of the vehicle's full-beam headlamps. Then she made him out, sitting behind the wheel of that pick-up. It was her husband Randy.

She exited the Honda silently and swiftly. So fast, in fact, that her husband had only one foot on the ground when he saw his wife.

Her finger was itching to press the trigger. But she wanted to take one long last look at him before she said goodbye for ever.

No words were exchanged between them. Harriet just saw him pan down to the shotgun in her hand and mouth the word "No!". That was all he had time to do before she allowed that itchy finger to get on with what it wanted to do.

She aimed right at his heart. It had to be the best place to start with. Harriet felt the weapon jolt in her hand as she fired. It must have lifted up a full five inches after the first cartridge shot out of the stubby barrel she had so painstakingly sawn down a few days earlier.

Randy Giesecke was thrown back a good three feet by the force of that first shot. It seared into his chest — a spray of tiny fragments of metal, each one piercing its own hole in the flesh. Instinctively, he put his right hand up to feel the gaping wound. If he had looked down at that moment he would have seen his shredded heart, barely pumping and exposed through the shattered remains of his chest.

Harriet Giesecke walked towards her husband then, determined to get a better aim before she blasted him into eternity. He was half-standing as the blood poured rapidly out of him. But she was not close enough yet.

Randy Giesecke looked up at the approaching death machine and let his eyelids flutter in resignation. He knew the end was very near. Now he just wanted her to get on with it, for he could not stand the pain a moment longer. All he could really see were the two barrels getting nearer and nearer. Harriet wanted him to suffer. Her upper lip curled as she witnessed his pain. So good to see. It inspired her to let that index finger do its job once again. This time the shot ripped open a hole in his head the size of a golfball.

Harriet headed for the Honda Accord. Just five floors above them in the same apartment block, little Erica was playing with her teddy bears as the baby-sitter watched the seven o'clock TV news.

Harriet Giesecke put on a marvellous performance at her slain husband's funeral in the nearby town of North York. The eyes of all his relatives were upon her as they lowered his body into the ground a week after what the newspapers called a "senseless, cold-blooded robbery attempt that had gone tragically wrong".

She was enjoying every minute of their suffering.

160

At least now Randy would not get to have custody of Erica, even if she was still deemed far too irresponsible to look after the child herself.

As she drove away from the funeral, having been snubbed by all her husband's relatives, Harriet was feeling good about life for the first time in years. If she had paid better attention to her rear-view mirror, she might have seen the two plain-clothes-police squad cars following her through the streets of North York.

She did not even notice them when she stopped in Edwards Gardens, walked over to an empty bench and waited for her secret lover to turn up for a clandestine meeting.

Across the street, Bruce Lynch walked casually towards her without even bothering to question why two saloon cars, each filled with three men, were stationed just a hundred yards from where his girlfriend was patiently waiting.

The detectives could not believe their luck. All fingers were pointing towards Harriet Giesecke as the main suspect in the murder of her husband, but so far they did not have a shred of evidence against her. As the officers watched the so-called grieving widow sitting with a man on that wooden bench, passionately kissing him, their eyebrows arched and they knew they were onto something.

Harriet, for her part, was just relieved to be close to Bruce once more. Their illicit sex sessions in places as obscure as the floor under her bed when they were together in the Clarke Institute were now just a fond memory. As she felt his lips kissing her neck, she wished she could just pull him down on top of her in that very public place. But not even Harriet Giesecke could bring herself to be that outrageous.

As she ran her fingers through his thick black hair, she could not wait to get him to herself. It would not be long, and then they could be together for ever.

The detectives witnessing the couple's passion on that bench were intrigued. What was Harriet doing with a parole violator with a long history of armed robbery? They knew there and then that it would only be a matter of time before they arrested Harriet Giesecke for the murder of her husband.

And Harriet's romantic escapades on a park bench were not the only interesting facts unearthed by detectives over the next few days. A cashier at a sports shop in the nearby Newtonbrook Plaza recalled Harriet coming into the store looking for a high-powered magnum "Dirty Harry" special, plus ammunition, to hunt "big game". That was just a few days before the murder of Randy Giesecke.

Then a nursery-school teacher came forward to tell cops that she had seen Harriet Giesecke driving a car into the underground car park of the apartment block where her husband and daughter lived. She recalled the precise time — it had been 6.15pm, about an hour before Randy was blasted to death so cold-bloodedly.

The jigsaw was complete when police searched the flat Harriet shared with her lover Bruce and found a saw and fragments of metal that came from the remains of the shotgun when she cut it down for maximum killing potential.

Two months after her husband's vicious slaying, Harriet Giesecke was arrested and charged with his murder.

On the last day of her trial, June 18, 1988, Giesecke was so confident she would be found not guilty that she turned to one of the cops guarding her, held up her handcuffed wrists and said: "This is the last time you'll be putting these cuffs on me."

After the jury deliberated for more than four days, Giesecke was astonished to be found guilty of first-degree murder. Her lover Bruce Lynch was acquitted of all involvement in the crime.

Harriet Giesecke is currently serving her life sentence

in the Kingston Penitentiary for Women, with no eligibility for parole for at least twenty-five years. Ironically, her lover Bruce Lynch is serving a ten-year sentence for robbery and theft at the nearby Joyceville Penitentiary.

The couple were given special permission to marry in June, 1989, in Harriet's prison. Authorities were especially amazed by their decision to wed because Harriet had tried to implicate Lynch in the murder of her husband.

But, every six weeks, armed guards bring Lynch to visit Harriet at her jail and they are allowed to spend at least two hours in a trailer in the prison grounds. It is believed the couple enjoy a full marriage.

Meanwhile, Harriet's daughter Erica — now 7 years old — is living happily and securely with Randy Giesecke's parents in Toronto. Harriet has told people she misses her daughter "very much" but it is unlikely they will ever meet again if the Giesckes have any say in the matter.

11

The Root Of All Evil

The noise of aircraft taking off from nearby Heathrow Airport every thirty seconds is the sound that dominates life in Hounslow, Middlesex. It is a somewhat sad, sprawling concrete jungle of high-rise estates and tatty between-the-wars housing that can be seen from any aircraft approaching Britain's busiest travel centre.

Not surprisingly, property prices have always been fairly reasonable in Hounslow. It is stuck in that no man's land between the city and the countryside. And, for that reason, it became probably one of the most popular areas in Britain for the teeming masses of Asian immigrants who flooded into the country in the fifties and sixties.

These were hard-working people who dreamt of opening shops and businesses, and living the sort of lifestyles many of them knew they could never attain in their homeland. And certainly, without the hundreds of thousands of immigrants from countries like India and Pakistan, this country's individually owned shops might have become a thing of the past, as the huge supermarket chains swallowed up customers at an alarming rate.

So, the majority of shops in Hounslow were naturally owned by those very same hard-working Asians. Many of these businesses stayed open virtually throughout the night and, as a result, earned their owners healthy profits compared with their British predecessors, who tended to run rigid nine-to-five operations.

The other reason why the Asian population of places like Hounslow did such good business was that most of their shops were manned by members of their own families. Wives, sons, daughters, mothers and fathers were all expected to do their stint behind the counter. These shopkeepers were never saddled with the expense of hiring staff — they were already living on the premises.

Mohinder Cheema was one such classic example of a successful Asian businessman in Hounslow. Since arriving in Britain in the fifties, he had gradually bought up an off-licence, two shops and a host of other residential property at a time when prices were but a mere fraction of what they are today.

But no-one — not even his attractive dark-haired wife Julie — knew exactly how much Mohinder Cheema was worth. The 54-year-old businessman kept things close to his chest. It was frustrating for all those around him, like Julie and the three children they had between them. But that was the way Mohinder had always operated and nothing was going to change his habit of a lifetime.

Sometimes, 44-year-old Julie Cheema wondered why she had married her husband in the first place. Their romance and eventual wedding in 1985 had surprised both their families. He was the frail, yet astute millionaire who had carefully and patiently nurtured a whole range of businesses in the area. She came from a much more traditional British background and many people found it hard to imagine what on earth they could have in common.

But Julie was very taken with her husband at first. He had a wonderful eye for a deal. An ability to make money out of nothing, and she really respected that skill in any man. But that kind of admiration is not usually enough to keep a marriage intact.

There was another side to her husband that most women would find hard to cope with. The physical side of their relationship was virtually non-existent. Mohinder Cheema suffered from chronic asthma and frequently had to retire to bed when his breathing became seriously affected.

At first, Julie was a sympathetic nurse. Helping and understanding her husband's obvious suffering. But after a few years of marriage, she started to resent

165

the constant interruptions to her life. She longed for the physical side of their marriage to get going now and again. But somehow she knew that they could never have a normal marriage in the accepted sense. Julie Cheema began to look elsewhere for affection.

Neil Marklew was a gangly youth of just 19 when he first met Julie. To begin with, this unlikely twosome became genuine friends. There was no physical bond between them. After all, he was twenty-five years younger than her. But, despite the age difference, Neil and Julie had a lot in common. He lived with his parents in Catherine Gardens, just around the corner from the Cheemas' main off-licence in Cromwell Road, Hounslow.

Naturally, they met when he used to pop into the shop for some ice-cold beers to take home. The first few times they had just exchanged pleasantries. He did not even really notice her hand brush his as she gave him change. He certainly did not realise that she was building him up into the object of her desires.

But then Julie Cheema did not have much else in her life at that time. Her husband was becoming more and more short-tempered as his asthma attacks became increasingly regular.

However, there was an even more disturbing development in the Cheema household: Mohinder Cheema was beginning to make all sorts of thinly veiled threats to his wife about cutting her out of his will. He might have been a sick man, but he knew full well that his wife was not truly in love with him. His children from his earlier marriage did not get on with her and they kept warning him. Inevitably, he began to take heed of their advice. He started to question her motives in even having married him in the first place. He wondered what her real intentions were.

The relationship between Julie and her husband had reached an all-time low by the summer of 1990.

Business might have been going extremely well in the Cheema store, but life at home was just one long round of arguments and tension. Mohinder Cheema was spending much of his time in bed and his wife was trying to stay out of the house as frequently as possible.

Then one day she came home early and was about to enter his bedroom when she heard voices. It was one of his grown-up sons. She stopped in her tracks and waited and listened. The voices were loud and clear. They were discussing Mohinder's will, and it was becoming perfectly clear that there were plans afoot to cut Julie out of it.

She waited a few moments longer and then silently tiptoed away. She did not want them to know she had been listening, because she was about to hatch a plan that had to be completely foolproof.

Neil Marklew knew that Julie Cheema had a soft spot for him and he was enjoying the attention of an older woman. They would meet in the middle of the day whilst her husband was working in the shop. Neil — unemployed — enjoyed their little love trysts because it broke up the monotony of his life on the dole. The days were the most boring time of all because so many of his mates were either at college or out working.

During that hot summer of 1990, they met in parks, pubs and coffee shops to talk about life, love and Mohinder Cheema. Julie seemed almost obsessed with her husband and his plans to cut her out of the will. She knew he had not done it yet, but she firmly believed it would happen. She knew full well that her husband was watching her every move. He suspected she was getting physical gratification from elsewhere. The truth was that Julie had not committed adultery — yet. She was more content just having a companion to confide in, even if he was young enough to be her son.

But, as is so often the case, teenager Neil Marklew's affection for Julie was growing by the day. He found himself thinking about her virtually every waking moment. The more they met and talked, the more he began to want her all to himself. Yet, up until then, they had done nothing more than kiss on street corners and stroke hands over the tops of coffee-shop tables.

Virtually no-one knew about their secret liaisons. Neil knew that his mates would rib him mercilessly if they found out, and Julie certainly had no intention of telling a living soul. But Neil was starting to feel completely swept up by her. He was prepared to do anything to encourage their love — her wishes were his commands.

"I'd kill him for you if you asked me."

Neil Marklew was fooling around with his 44-year-old sweetheart. He just wanted to show her how much he cared for her. But Julie Cheema took it all the wrong way.

"Do you mean that?"

The teenager hesitated for a moment and looked into Julie Cheema's eyes. He had a horrible feeling she was taking him seriously. But he wanted to show her just how tough he was — it was the biggest mistake he ever made in his entire life.

"Sure I do," he mumbled. But she took no notice of his reticence.

"I hate him, you know. I've been thinking of killing him for ages but I don't know how."

Neil Marklew had opened up a whole can of worms and now he was discovering what it would take to win Julie's love for ever.

He sat there nodding his head as she took a deep breath and carried on:

"There must be a way we could do it."

Neil was starting to get used to the idea. He began to realise that this might be a way out of the doldrums of unemployment. His love for her was blinded by emotion. Just so long as they were careful, then why should they get caught?

"Well, it'll cost you."

"How much do you think?"

"You tell me — what's he worth?"

"Five million."

Neil let out a long whistle. He had no idea his sweetheart's husband was worth that sort of money.

"I'd just be happy to run the off-licence."

"Okay. It's yours if you do the job properly."

The truth was that Julie Cheema had always had an inflated opinion of her husband's real wealth. But to her, one off-licence seemed a small price to pay compared to the five million pounds she believed he was worth in total. In reality, it was about one fifth of that sum.

"Right, give me some money and I'll get a gun."

Neil also knew just the bloke for this job of assassin.

Robert Naughton, aged 20, was desperate for money. Like his friend Neil Marklew, he was also unemployed but he did not have the luxury of his parents to fall back on. He needed cash fast and when his pal suggested a "little job" he did not hesitate. Even when Neil passed him the sawn-off shotgun and told him the victim was his sweetheart's husband, he did not bat an eyelid.

As far as Naughton was concerned, it would be a "piece of cake". The two friends finished off their pints of bitter in their local tavern and walked out to prepare for the job that they hoped would set them up with a business for life.

"Bang. Bang." Neil turned to his pal: "It'll be as easy as that."

It was a pretty hot day in Hounslow in August, 1990. Business in cold drinks was brisk at the Cheemas' off-licence in Cromwell Road and Mohinder Cheema must have been hoping the good weather would continue.

169

He and his wife were both in the shop during the late afternoon that day, as was so often the case. Julie was giving the place a good clean and her husband was sitting — due to his bad health — behind the counter of the shop.

Neither of them paid much attention to a gangly youth who walked in. Perhaps if they had bothered to look at him a bit sooner, they would have noticed that he was wearing a heavy coat despite the scorching hot weather.

By the time Robert Naughton pulled out his shotgun, it was too late.

The first shower of metal hit Mohinder Cheema in the side of his chest. As he keeled over on the floor, Naughton pointed and fired a second time. On this occasion, the fragments of shot somehow missed most of their target except for Mohinder Cheema's fingers. Doctors later found lots of pieces of shot embedded in his hands.

Julie turned and screamed as she saw Naughton standing there with the gun. It was pretty convincing.

Naughton then fled as Mohinder Cheema lay groaning on the floor. Julie rushed to her husband's side. She looked down at the bloody mess sprawled on the ground and saw that he was still very much alive, despite the cold-blooded attack.

She tried not to look too disappointed. She wondered if maybe the shots would have their desired effect if she just left him there bleeding for a few minutes. She looked outside at Naughton as he made off into the distance and then started crying.

"Oh my God! Mohinder! Oh my God!"

It was an Oscar-winning performance. Two of his children rushed down the stairs from the flat above to help. Meanwhile Julie Cheema ever so slowly called the ambulance service. She did not want them to be too fast, just in case the delay was long enough for her husband to bleed to death.

Mohinder Cheema miraculously survived that attack. As Julie held her husband's hand in the ambulance while it rushed to a nearby hospital, she must have been praying he would die. The ambulance crew looked on, in sympathy with the victim's wife. The wives were usually the ones who did most of the suffering. But in the case of Julie Cheema, grieving was just an act of deceit.

She had a horrible feeling that her husband was going to survive — and that would mean starting her plans all over again. This time they must not fail. Her tears were filled with disappointment, not fear. She had willed him to die but he clearly would not go that easily.

The shooting of Mohinder Cheema created quite a stir in the newspapers that week. The so-called expert crime reporters of the national press were running serious in-depth pieces on the Asian mafia-style gangs that were believed to have gunned down the off-licence owner because he refused to pay protection money.

Reports that the gunman was Asian-looking just helped add fuel to the fire. Neighbours in Cromwell Road were said to be in deep shock about the shooting. Respectable Indian and Pakistani shopkeepers spoke in great detail about their run-ins with these notorious gangs.

Even Julie Cheema voiced her determination not to bow down to these hoods who had so nearly taken away the life of her dearly beloved husband.

"I haven't paid and I won't pay. I work seven days a week and I won't hand over any of my hard-earned money."

The headline in the *Daily Mail* that day was: CORNER SHOP WIFE DEFIES THE MOBSTERS.

Yet, in a bizarre sort of way, Julie Cheema was telling the truth. However, it was her husband whom she suspected of trying to take what was rightfully hers.

Meanwhile, in Charing Cross Hospital, Mohinder Cheema underwent emergency surgery that was simply postponing the death sentence that had already been passed on him.

He had one of his kidneys removed and one of his fingers amputated. He was hailed as a hero in the local press. In fact, the whole incident had some great benefits for Mohinder Cheema. He had become a bit of a local celebrity in his battle to stave off the brutal hitmen from the Asian racketeers.

The millionaire businessman was so convinced by all the publicity that he even hired a team of bodyguards to protect him when he was released from hospital. He was worried about his wife's safety back at the off-licence as well. He even told her to be very careful if she worked there alone. Julie Cheema smiled at him and told him not to worry. She knew full well the gangs were but a figment of his imagination. But she couldn't help chuckling to herself when she realised she had sparked off a feeling of fear in the Asian community. Other killings and shootings of shopkeepers throughout West London were being linked to the Mohinder Cheema case. If only they had known the truth from the outset.

Back in Hounslow, Julie Cheema was determined to make sure her husband was not so lucky a second time around. She was naturally concerned about his plans to hire bodyguards, as she knew it would make her job far more difficult.

Within days of that first shooting, she was scheming and plotting with Neil Marklew, who was still the key player in her plans. But this time, they had a distinct advantage because Mohinder Cheema was absent from the family home.

"This time, you better make sure he dies."

Julie Cheema could be fairly cold when she wanted to be. She was annoyed with her sweetheart's pal for failing to kill her husband first time around. But she

172

felt an even stronger affinity towards Neil. As they discussed how to make sure the plan really did work, she stroked his youthful face and leant over and kissed him full on the lips. When his tongue began probing her mouth in return, she knew that he would do anything for her.

"It has to be as soon as he gets home. I don't want any of those bodyguards getting in the way."

Never in a thousand dreams did Neil really expect to go to bed with Julie Cheema. She seemed so much older, so much more mature. He just could not imagine that their friendship would really blossom into all-out sex. But, as Mohinder Cheema lay close to death in hospital, Julie found she could no longer resist the temptation to bed her young friend.

In truth, she had craved his body since the first day they met, but she never had the opportunity to actually seal their lust for one another. But now, with her hubby out of the way, she had the perfect opportunity.

Neil Marklew was delighted that he was being taught some bedroom tricks by Julie. She was so much more experienced than anyone he had ever slept with before. He was perfectly happy to just lie back and let her take control.

As she straddled his body in her bedroom, she realised that he would do anything she commanded.

"You promise he won't miss this time?"

Neil Marklew's mind was on other things when his mature lover suddenly switched the conversation back to the inevitable — her husband.

"Of course I do. I promise you it will be done."

Julie Cheema continued having sex with her teenage lover and even allowed herself the luxury of a climax for the first time in years. She was really looking forward to the day when she could call all those businesses her own. That would teach her husband to try and cut her out of her will.

But first they had to wait for him to get out of hospital. For six long weeks, Julie Cheema continued her Academy Award-winning performances so as to convince her husband's family and the police that she had nothing whatsoever to do with the vicious attack on her husband.

She even went through the charade of visiting him in hospital. Taking him flowers and fruit as he lay there linked up to heart monitors and drips. She must have been sorely tempted to pull them out of their sockets and just walk calmly away from that room. But Julie knew that all fingers would point at her. No, she had the perfect cover of the Asian gangs out to kill her defiant husband. It was obvious that they would come after him again.

Julie Cheema was genuinely delighted when doctors told her that her husband could go home. It was October 3, 1990 — just six weeks after that first attack. Her happiness was sparked not by her husband's speedy recovery but by the expectation that soon he would be gone for ever. There was no time to waste, as the bodyguards he had hired would be in place the following day.

As she drove him back through West London to his pride and joy — that off-licence in Cromwell Road, Hounslow — she felt the twinge of nervous excitement building up inside. She kept telling him how glad she was that he had been released from hospital. How relieved she was that he had decided to hire minders. Mohinder Cheema looked at his wife in admiration. She really was bearing up to all the stresses and strains very well.

The journey back to their home took no more than forty-five minutes and, just as she knew he would, Mohinder Cheema insisted on taking a look around his off-licence before going off to bed to recuperate. As he walked around the shelves, still in his dressing-gown and slippers, inspecting the stock, she realised

174

why she was so glad he was about to be killed. He really was a fussy old man. He did not even trust her enough to let her carry on running the business without interfering. He wanted to know why they were short on stocks of certain brands of wine. She answered him charmingly. Her happiness was hard to contain because she knew that it would not be long now.

When she turned and saw the familiar figure of Robert Naughton approaching the shop, she slipped quietly behind the counter and waited impatiently. Come on. Come on. Let's just get it over and done with.

Just like before, Mohinder Cheema did not notice Naughton until it was too late. This time, he turned towards the gunman and then looked over at his wife standing silently nearby. Mohinder Cheema knew at that moment that she must have been behind it. He could tell from that nervous expression on her lips as he turned to stare death in the face.

Robert Naughton blasted both shots right at his head this time. Basically, he could not fail. Mohinder Cheema's 18-year-old son Sunil — who had just walked into the shop — only realised what was happening when it was too late. If he had turned and seen it coming a few moments earlier, he might have seen that look on his step-mother's face.

The shots hit Mohinder in the back of the head and the neck. There was no way he could survive them this time. He was dead as soon as he hit the floor.

As his son rushed next door to a neighbour to raise the alarm, Julie Cheema leant down and looked over her husband's injured body for the second time in less than two months. But she could tell immediately that her lover and his friend had succeeded. A warm smile came to her lips and she stood up and walked towards the front of the shop, trying hard to force a sob and a tear to well up in her eyes.

Mohinder Cheema lay there in a pool of blood, still

175

wearing the Charing Cross Hospital dressing-gown he
had been wearing when he arrived at the shop just
fifteen minutes earlier.

Julie Cheema was found guilty of murder and attempted
murder when she appeared in front of a jury at the
Old Bailey in July, 1991. Her lover Neil Marklew
and his friend Robert Naughton admitted murder and
attempted murder. All three were given life sentences.
  Detectives admitted that if it had not been for the
testimony of Neil Marklew, Mrs Cheema might never
have been arrested.
  Her son Kismat, aged 18, was given three months'
youth custody for conspiring to murder Mohinder
Cheema.

12
The Bigamist Must Die

Her face was vibrant. Neat, smooth features somehow made even more attractive by the straight bridge of her Roman nose. Then there were her eyes. Dark seas of diamonds. Glistening with an intriguing combination of vitality and animal cunning. When she looked at people, the lids would narrow slightly. They held a magnetism that was almost hypnotic. Even her long, flowing dark hair was eye-catching as the neon lights bounced off her head like a sun setting behind a mountain.

Then there were her breasts. Firm, ample, shapely. Pointing straight ahead so as to catch the eye of any passing admirer. They clung to the silky blouse that was undone just enough to reveal a hint of bosom. Her bottom was just as well designed. A definite curve, yet still retaining the delicate look that made men want to pat it ever so gently. Her legs were covered in black stockings that night. The skirt began two inches above the knee. They hinted at her sexuality, but not so much that it might put any man off the goods on offer. Her whole appearance was geared around her persona — sultry, sexual and very, very luscious.

William Nelson was transfixed by her as she stood at the bar of a small tavern in Costa Mesa, California, that evening in the winter of 1991. He did not know her name or anything about her, but he could not keep his eyes off her. Every now and again she turned and smiled ever so slightly. But he could not be sure if it was a come-on or wishful thinking on his part. In any case, what would a truly beautiful 23-year-old woman be doing trying to tempt a haggard 56-year-old? No, thought William, it must be my imagination. He returned to his beer, delighted to be enjoying his liberty again after just being released from a long spell inside.

177

William could not get that girl out of his mind. Every time he looked up she was still there, gazing over in his direction. He tried to avert his eyes, watch the other people in the bar. Next to him, three bikers were discussing the inner workings of their Harley Davidsons. Over at the other end of the bar, a couple seemed deeply engrossed in some emotional upheaval or other. Across the way, three gaudy girls giggled and laughed and caught his eye the instant he looked in their direction. William looked away hastily; he had seen two of those women on a lot of occasions before in that bar and he knew they were definitely the types to avoid. Two of them had their own slinky dress code that consisted of stone-washed skin-tight jeans and razor-sharp stilettos. On that particular night, the other one — a strawberry blonde — had on a black and white checked pair of hotpants that were so short and so tight you could see the seam of her tights, as well as the separated cheeks of her bottom. William knew that, however desperate he might be for a woman, those three were to be avoided.

Then his eyes panned around once more in the direction of that mystery girl, sitting all alone at the bar. This time she had crossed her legs as she sat on a stool. It had the desirable effect of hitching up her skirt a further three, or maybe even four, inches to reveal a full pair of thighs that were very much enhanced by their covering of black stocking. William could just make out the seams of those stockings as they travelled from her neat, trim ankles up and up into the shadow above her thighs that old men could only dream about.

This time he looked up and definitely caught a look of recognition. There was no doubting it. William felt a shiver of expectation run through his body. She was a very attractive woman and she seemed interested in him...

Omaima Stainbrook was well aware of the probing,

lusting eyes of William Nelson feasting upon her very trim body as she sat at that bar. But she never liked to hurry herself. She knew full well that if she made it too easy for him then he might just take her for a prostitute, and she was looking for a long-term relationship not some cheap and nasty sex followed by an instant dismissal.

Omaima was just 23 years old, but she had already led a pretty full life. She knew exactly how to tempt and titillate men, and William was about to join a long list of useful admirers.

But before she even talked to him, she wanted to tease and tantalise him some more. She swung her stool around a few inches, so that she was virtually facing him, and took a long drag of her cigarette before opening her legs just a fraction. She could feel his eyes longing for her now. It was a good feeling. She always enjoyed those first few minutes when the hunt was in its preliminary stages. There was something very exciting about knowing that a complete stranger was lusting after you. But then Omaima was looking for something much more than a mere tease.

She pulled her lipstick out of her handbag and pressed it firmly against the edge of her mouth. With her mirror in one hand and the lipstick in the other, she wiped the stick across and then back over her lips. Slowly, ever so slowly, she held the rounded end of the lipstick to her lips for a moment and glanced casually in William Nelson's direction. She smiled as their eyes caught each other.

Within seconds, the lipstick was back in the handbag and William Nelson was making his first tentative effort to approach this beautiful creature of the night.

"Hi. Would you like a drink?"

William did not know what else to say. He might have spent quite a few years in jail, but he was not some hardened criminal. His offences were things like

179

smuggling electronic goods into Mexico, and the odd bit of dope. Throughout all his jail terms, he had always retained a truly gentlemanly manner — and that night was no exception.

"No. I've got one, thanks."

Omaima was not going to make it that easy for William. She wanted him to make a real effort to catch her, then she would know that he was serious and not some married man out to get an easy lay.

She took out a cigarette and put it to her lips slowly, almost sensuously, and waited. At first, William was so nervous he did not think to offer her a light. Then she parted two fingers and put them up to the filter. Suddenly it clicked.

William grappled for his lighter and, almost shaking with excitement, held it just steady enough to ignite her cigarette.

"Thanks."

She purred the word in such a way that William knew it was now or never. He had to start up a conversation before the silence killed off her lust for him instantly.

Within a few minutes they were sharing drinks and laughter as he told her about himself, neatly avoiding the obvious questions about being married and material wealth. Ironically, they were the two subjects dearest to Omaima's heart.

But she was not deterred. William was well dressed. He had a certain poise and confidence and he was wearing plenty of gold jewellery. Omaima reckoned she might be onto a good thing with William Nelson, and he certainly had no idea of the risks he was taking by even considering her as a partner.

Only a year earlier, Huntington Beach resident Robert Hanson had found himself embroiled with Omaima Stainbrook after a very similar encounter. The middle-aged clerk was clearly enchanted and flattered by the attentions of the beautiful young Egyptian-born immigrant and within a few weeks of meeting they had moved in together to his luxury apartment just near the Pacific Ocean.

It was a dream come true for Omaima. The sort of home that she could never have dreamt of owning all those years earlier when she was virtually destitute and living on the streets of Cairo.

Now she was engaged to be married to an elderly Californian who would ensure that she never had to return to that awful life that drove her into the arms of Mother America in the first place. The United States is the place of dreams for millions of people around the world, but for Omaima it was now a reality and she was determined to have herself the best life possible. But without a job, the only way to that fantasy world was with the help of men. She had discovered at an early age that her striking beauty could get her places. Men would literally fall at her feet. They would do anything for her.

Robert Hanson was just one such man in a long line of elderly males that Omaima tempted. She had learnt a long time ago that she was capable of doing anything to get what she wanted.

But when Robert had refused to marry Omaima it sparked off a fury inside her that was virtually uncontainable. Her only purpose in sleeping with Robert and moving into his house was to get him to marry her. Then she knew she was guaranteed an income for life. It was her way of ensuring she never had to return to the streets of Cairo again.

When he told her that he could not possibly marry her, despite the fact they had been living together for some months, she went crazy with anger. The feeling of betrayal built up so quickly within her that she could hardly stop herself shaking with rage. And when Robert Hanson returned one evening from a hard day at the office, she pulled a knife on him and locked him in the bedroom while she rifled through his wallet for all the money she could find. She knew it was

181

time to leave him because her plan had failed. But first she wanted to get what she believed was rightfully hers. When she could find only a few dollars in loose change, Omaima got even crazier and went after her live-in lover with the knife. He survived the attack and, too embarrassed at first to report it to the police, allowed Omaima to leave quietly.

Meanwhile she had sworn never to let any man sleep with her until they were married. That way, she wouldn't have that same problem ever again.

Now, back in that bar in Costa Mesa, she was about to ensnare another middle-aged man. But this time she would not waste her time living with him. This was marriage or nothing. But even Omaima knew that if she pushed for marriage within a few minutes of meeting William Nelson in that bar, it might scare him off. Instead, she allowed his hand to travel up that shapely thigh of hers as they sat together and just smiled a warm sensuous smile that convinced William that he was onto something good. But then the ex-convict had a few secrets of his own. And he was already so besotted by this dark-haired beauty that he did not give them even a moment's consideration as they stared into each other's eyes.

"What can you possibly see in me?"

It seemed a perfectly reasonable question for an ageing man to ask a shapely young temptress. Omaima blushed heavily and ran her hand gently up the inside of his trouser leg before digging her long nails into his flesh.

"You're so strong, William. I need your strength to guide me through life."

Unfortunately, William Nelson interpreted Omaima's words as a plea from the heart. The truth was that she was doing the devil's work and she still had a long way to go before she achieved her goal.

As he leant against her firm breasts and kissed her full, luscious glossy lips, all he could feel was the moisture of her tongue as it returned his gesture. He felt sure he could feel the electricity between them instantly.

Omaima allowed her tongue to probe the inner workings of his mouth without even giving it much consideration. An initial French kiss was but a small price to pay to entrap William Nelson in her weird world. The next stage might prove altogether more difficult.

Omaima's eyes positively lit up when he gave her a lift home in his gleaming red Corvette sports car. She had long since picked up that American habit of judging people by the car they drove, and William Nelson had just passed with flying colours.

She sat back and felt the warm November wind flow through her hair as he accelerated out of the parking lot with that powerful V8 engine virtually at full thrust. She would let him drop her off at her place and just allow him a goodnight kiss — nothing more at this early stage. She certainly did not want to appear to be an easy lay. She just wanted to let him know she was interested. That would be enough to have the desired effect.

"But I cannot sleep in the same bed as you unless we are married."

Omaima was most insistent. William Nelson might have been smitten by this beautiful woman, but he was expecting to have sex with her by the time they had been out on their third date. She had other plans.

"It is against my religious beliefs. I just cannot do it."

William was disappointed but not deterred. He had known Omaima just a few days but he had felt they were getting so close that making love together seemed only natural. He had suppressed his sexual appetite for long enough whilst in jail. Now, he had been out a few months, and he planned to take every opportunity that came his way.

"But here in the States it doesn't matter."

"It might not matter to you, William, but I still have very strong beliefs. I must stick to them."

William looked at his girlfriend and smiled. She was positively oozing with sensuality even as they sat there on the couch in his flat, talking. He had hardly been able to take his eyes off her since the first moment they met. He had even fantasised about what he wanted to do to her, as he lay in bed alone after that first meeting. He had memorised every inch of her body. He had imagined all the things they would do together. But now he was faced with the reality of the situation. She was saying they could not sleep together unless they were married. He knew he could not marry her. For a start, it seemed crazy to wed a girl just a few days after meeting — and then there was Katherine, over in Santa Maria, just fifty miles away. She might not be too pleased about it. After all, she was still his wife.

William was in a dilemma. He wanted this gorgeous young thing so badly that he would do anything to have her. He had never felt so tempted by a woman in all his life. He put his hands around her trim waist as they stood there in the hallway of his flat and hugged her tight. So tightly, in fact, that he did not feel the stiff tension running through her body. She only began to relax a little when he talked.

"Well, I must be crazy but I don't think I can live without you. Will you marry me?"

William Nelson did not know what had come over him. But he just had to have her.

Omaima did not even bother to reply. She just nodded her head and buried her face in his chest, smiling ever so discreetly to herself as she felt his hand travel up the back of her tight-fitting skirt. In the space of just a few days she had achieved precisely what she set out to do.

The wedding was a simple affair as marriages go. But

then Omaima did not mind. She just looked down at that certificate and breathed a huge sigh of relief. It had taken her just seven days from the moment she first met William Nelson. She looked over at the slightly crumpled figure of the 56-year-old man she had just agreed to make her husband and realised that marriage was a very small sacrifice to make, under the circumstances. She was certain he had some money and a visible means of supporting her. Now the whole scene was set.

She had fixed herself firmly into a position where a man was supporting her and would continue to do so for the rest of her life. As they boarded a plane on the afternoon of their wedding to go on honeymoon to Laredo, Texas, she was feeling very pleased with herself.

But William Nelson had other things on his mind during that trip. It was supposed to be the ultimate confirmation of their love for one another and, on that first night, William was indeed delighted when he finally got to sleep with Omaima. The sex might have been a little one-sided but she still looked sensational as she lay there waiting for him to join her in their hotel bed.

As he feasted on every inch of her body, she returned his passion vaguely. She was more excited by the thought of that nice apartment back in Costa Mesa and how she was going to completely redecorate it when they got back after the honeymoon. William did not really notice that his new wife's mind was on other things. The act of sex was a great way to escape the worries of the world for a few lustful minutes, and that was the way William looked at it. The business pressures were mounting and even the trip to Laredo had an ulterior purpose.

The Texas city's busy little airport had become the epicentre of his smuggling empire. It was just a short hop into Mexico, and William had become one of the most powerful smugglers of cheap electrical goods into the Central American nation that has always craved products of every size and shape from its fabulously wealthy neighbour — the US.

The trouble was that his lucrative business had been neglected during his most recent spell in prison and he needed desperately to build up the smuggling operation once more. That meant meetings with shady characters on isolated stretches of desert. It also meant leaving Omaima alone at their hotel for huge chunks of their honeymoon.

Still, at least she knew he was in business. Even if she did not realise just how illicit his work was. But all those long lonely hours at the hotel did enable Omaima to search through her brand new husband's belongings to find out more about him. With all the secrets she hid, it was only natural that she should suspect the man she had entrapped of having a few of his own.

But what she eventually found made her even madder than Robert Hanson had when he refused to marry her the previous year in Huntington Beach.

Omaima could not quite believe her eyes when she looked at the snapshot she had found in her new husband's jacket pocket. He was posing happily with a motherly-looking woman in her forties. It was clearly taken in recent months. He even had on the same shirt he had been wearing that first night they met in the Costa Mesa bar. But the most insulting thing was that he looked so happy.

She knew instinctively that this had to be someone very special in William's life. There was something about their closeness in that photograph that gave it all away. His arm was around this other woman, holding her tight. If Omaima's worst fears were confirmed, then her whole marriage scheme might have been a complete waste of time. Her intention had been to lure William into a relationship that was legally signed and sealed so that she was financially secure for life.

She tried to stop herself thinking about the possibility he was still married to this other woman. No, perhaps this was just some recent girlfriend. That must the answer, she thought to herself. But she had a nagging doubt about the whole business. She decided to confront William the moment he returned from his latest round of business meetings in Laredo.

"But I've filed for divorce. It's no big deal."

William Nelson was as cool as a cucumber when his pretty young bride confronted him with the evidence. He said that as far as he was concerned, his relationship with Katherine Nelson was over — dead and buried many months previously.

But Omaima was not so sure. Her own naturally inbuilt sense of paranoia was taking over now. She had been scheming all along during her relationship with William, but now the ball was on the other foot. She had discovered one of his secrets — and it was threatening to put paid to her dreams of an easy life of leisure.

"I don't believe you...you look so happy in the photo."

"You have to believe me. I wouldn't lie to you."

But that just wasn't a good enough reply for Omaima. She had been lied to and tricked all through her adult life. Why should she suddenly start trusting someone now? The world was out to get her and she was wreaking her own bizarre form of revenge.

She decided to accept what he was saying, for the moment, while she tried to work out an alternative plan. She knew that if William was still married to Katherine and anything happened to him, then she would get nothing. All those nights of sex she had endured. All those boring evenings listening to him droning on as his whiskey-sodden breath wafted across the table at her. All those awful moments when she pretended to return his lust. It would all turn out to have been a complete waste of time unless he was married to her. Legally.

187

On the flight back to California they hardly spoke. She was seething with fury. She still feared that he might have another wife. They had long since stopped talking about it, but William Nelson knew full well what his gorgeous young wife was thinking. He appreciated her distress but, as far as he was concerned, she was just a rather insecure young bride.

Over the next two or three weeks, Omaima tried to put the "other wife" out of her mind as she went about her chores in the Costa Mesa flat. William was often out, working his shady deals, so she took advantage of his absences to stamp her mark on the home they shared.

She had grandiose plans for redecorating the flat, buying better furniture and even laying new beige carpet. But first she set about the task of cleaning it from top to bottom. The trouble was that every few hours she would come across yet more evidence of William's other wife. It was distressing her for all the wrong reasons, and she was starting to wonder if Katherine Nelson had ever visited her husband at that very same apartment, even though William insisted they had been apart for a long period of time.

Every night William came home she would cook him a huge meal but the sparkle had definitely gone out of their relationship. She found it difficult to talk to him and he was well aware that she was still mad at him because of Katherine.

It was about four weeks after their wedding that Omaima realised she could not stand to live a lie any longer. As she cleaned up the apartment yet again and awaited the return of the man she had thought was going to be her saviour just one short month earlier, she felt a surge of fury building through her body like nothing she had ever experienced before. It was even worse than the way she had felt when she attacked Robert Hanson a year earlier in Huntington Beach.

188

When William Nelson put his key in the front door of their flat as he arrived home that evening, it was like a signal to Omaima. She grabbed the six-inch carving knife off the work surface and walked straight towards the hallway. As her husband walked in, he froze. The blade was pointing right at him.

Omaima did not bother to wait for him to plead for his life. She plunged the knife right into his chest as he stood there in shock at the sight of his deranged wife. The first stab was delivered with all the strength she could muster. For good measure, she twisted the blade round and round to cause maximum damage. It had the desired effect.

William Nelson collapsed on the floor clutching his stomach, where the wound must have been the size of a tennis ball. Then Omaima calmly stood over him for a moment before looking down in disdain at the writhing bigamist who was now at her complete mercy.

She bent over him and looked deep into his eyes. They were cesspools of fear now. Glazed with terror as he saw the bloodied knife in her hand. At one point he tried to clutch her but ended up swiping through thin air because his sight was misty and unclear.

His attempt to stop her just enflamed her determination to finish him off. She lashed that knife through his shoulder blade. Over and over again she struck. After each wound was inflicted he gasped for air as the bubbles of blood started to come up in his throat. Omaima felt no emotion or pain as she rained that knife down on him. Her only thoughts were to avenge his deception and on how she would get rid of the butchered corpse.

Omaima tried to keep her eyes averted from the task at hand as she sliced through the tender flesh. She knew that if she looked down at her husband's corpse, then she might be sick. And that would mean more to clear up. As it was, she had him laid out on the floor over plastic bin liners so that the blood did not seep through onto the heads of the tenants in the flat below.

Strangely enough, the longer she was there carving away the easier it became. After dislodging each limb, she placed it in one of the four trash bags she was gradually filling up. In many ways, this was the easy part. Carrying the squelching bags down to the car would be a far riskier operation, as she would inevitably encounter other residents of the apartment complex and that might prove a little tricky.

The head was the last piece of her husband's body to be placed gently in one of those extra strong bin bags. She was surprised by the weight of it. She tried hard not to look at it but she could not resist one glance as she held it right out in front of her so as to avoid getting blood on her dress. He looked oddly content as he stared back at her. There might even have been a smile on his stiff, blue lips. She stopped for a moment and blinked her eyes. It almost seemed as if he had winked at her. It was only when she opened and closed her eyes quickly that she realised it was just an illusion.

As she tied the top of that last bin bag tightly and lifted it up to begin the journey out to her husband's shining red Corvette sports car in the underground garage, she did not even notice the nosy neighbour from across the hall eyeing the drip of blood that was coming from one of the split bags. That same resident had heard a man's screams a few hours earlier but thought nothing of it, as there were quite a few strange people living in the block. But when he saw the bin bags and the blood, he knew something was seriously wrong. His fears were further confirmed when Omaima appeared to have blood still on her arms. The police were on the scene within minutes...

Omaima Nelson is currently being held without bail at the Orange County Jail charged with the murder of her husband. A few weeks after her arrest, in December, 1991, she was also charged with imprisoning and attempting to rob Robert Hanson at the apartment they had shared in Huntington Beach, California.